The .... hithe-
atre in ....

In the last glow of the evening Sabra's hair, against the bare stone, seemed to shine as if it held the light of the sun.

As the Marquis stood looking at her, he saw that tears were running down her cheeks.

Instinctively he put his arms around her and she turned her face against his shoulder.

The Marquis thought in the dying light that no one could be more lovely.

His lips came down on hers.

He overwhelmed her and his lips awoke in her strange feelings she had never known.

He kissed her fiercely, demandingly, as if he wanted to conquer her and make her completely and absolutely his prisoner...

A Camfield Novel of Love
by Barbara Cartland

"Barbara Cartland's novels are all distinguished by their intelligence, good sense, and good nature..."

— **ROMANTIC TIMES**

"Who could give better advice on how to keep your romance going strong than the world's most famous romance novelist, Barbara Cartland?"

— **THE STAR**

Camfield Place,
Hatfield
Hertfordshire,
England

Dearest Reader,

Camfield Novels of Love mark a very exciting era of my books with Jove. They have already published nearly two hundred of my titles since they became my first publisher in America, and now all my original paperback romances in the future will be published exclusively by them.

As you already know, Camfield Place in Hertfordshire is my home, which originally existed in 1275, but was rebuilt in 1867 by the grandfather of Beatrix Potter.

It was here in this lovely house, with the best view in the county, that she wrote *The Tale of Peter Rabbit*. Mr. McGregor's garden is exactly as she described it. The door in the wall that the fat little rabbit could not squeeze underneath and the goldfish pool where the white cat sat twitching its tail are still there.

I had Camfield Place blessed when I came here in 1950 and was so happy with my husband until he died, and now with my children and grandchildren, that I know the atmosphere is filled with love and we have all been very lucky.

It is easy here to write of love and I know you will enjoy the Camfield Novels of Love. Their plots are definitely exciting and the covers very romantic. They come to you, like all my books, with love.

Bless you,

CAMFIELD NOVELS OF LOVE
by Barbara Cartland

Other books by Barbara Cartland

A NEW CAMFIELD NOVEL OF LOVE BY

BARBARA CARTLAND

Starlight Over Tunis

JOVE BOOKS, NEW YORK

STARLIGHT OVER TUNIS

A Jove Book / published by arrangement with
the author

PRINTING HISTORY
Jove edition / October 1987

ISBN: 0-515-09213-4

Jove Books are published by The Berkley Publishing Group,
200 Madison Avenue, New York, New York 10016.
The name "JOVE" and the "J" logo
are trademarks belonging to Jove Publications, Inc.

PRINTED IN THE UNITED STATES OF AMERICA

10 9 8 7 6 5 4 3 2 1

Author's Note

I MOTORED with my son for a thousand miles over Tunisia and found it as beautiful, intriguing, and exciting as I have depicted it in this novel.

The mystery and atmosphere of the Amphitheatre at El Djem is difficult to put into words, just as the beauty of Tunisia and its Roman ruins is unforgettable.

After I had been there I wrote this poem about the feelings of the Roman women who lived there for so long, and had to make a home for their families far from their own people.

I felt their sadness and home-sickness still vibrating in the ruins of the Temples and Villas which will be forever Rome.

THE SOLDIER'S WIFE

Did you suffer in an alien land?
Did you weep at being far from Rome?
Did the conqueror's foot on miles of sand
Mean anything except it was not home?

The Romans won and lost the world.
The Greeks, the Goths, the French all fought
For power, while holy Spain unfurled
Horrors and cruelty of another sort.

So many broken lives, so many tears,
What does it mean in centuries to come?
Can broken pillars tell us of the fears
That women feel, while men still beat the drum?

chapter one

1897

THE Marquis of Quinbourne came out of his Villa onto the verandah and looked out over the Mediterranean.

The sun was just lifting the mist over the horizon and the view was breath-taking.

The Marquis, however, was deep in his own thoughts, when the window in the verandah opened and a vision appeared.

She was dressed in the height of fashion, but with a flamboyant *chic* which could only have been French.

"I have come to say *au revoir, Mon Cher,*" she said with a fascinating accent.

The Marquis rose slowly to his feet.

"The carriage is waiting for you, Jeanne, and

when you get to Monte Carlo, send it straight back."

"I will do that," Jeanne said.

She hesitated, then impulsively, with a flutter of her mascaraed eye-lashes and a pouting of her red mouth, she said very softly:

"*C'est très triste, Mon Cher,* that it should end like this."

"There is no reason for you to be sorry, Jeanne," the Marquis replied, "and thank you for all the happiness you have given me."

"Have you really been happy?"

"You have made me as happy as possible in the circumstances, and I can only regret that I have not been for you what you expected."

Jeanne shrugged her shoulders in a typically French gesture.

"*C'est la vie!*" she said, "but I did think when you asked me to stay that we should be very gay, and it would be amusing at the Casino in Monte Carlo, and in the fashionable places like *l' Hotel de Paris.*"

"I know, I know!" the Marquis said irritably. "But recriminations will get us nowhere."

He paused before he continued:

"I can only once again express my regrets and I hope, Jeanne, that the cheque I have made out in your name will be some compensation for having left Paris and so many gaieties behind."

It was then that a shrewd look came into Jeanne's dark eyes as she opened the envelope the

Marquis had given her and glanced at the contents.

The amount on the cheque made her draw in her breath, and she threw her arms round his neck, pulling his head down to hers.

"You are very kind, *très gentil! Merci, merci beaucoup!* Perhaps I should not leave you."

"No, you are right, completely right," the Marquis replied. "I have a great deal to think about, and I know you find it boring when I am thinking."

Jeanne laughed.

"That is true, and although at night you are a marvellous lover, in the daytime—oh-la-la!—it has been very, very dull!"

The Marquis laughed a little ruefully.

"I cannot dispute that, and you must forgive me, Jeanne, for inflicting my own troubles on you. Another time, I promise I will be different."

"Another time we will meet in Paris," Jeanne said positively. "In Paris you have always been everything a woman could want, but here, in this Villa..."

She made an eloquent little gesture with her hands, then once again her arms were round the Marquis's neck and she kissed him passionately on the mouth before she said:

"*Au revoir, Mon Cher,* but not *adieu,* for we shall meet again and perhaps very soon."

"In the meantime, I am sure you will be all right," the Marquis smiled.

"Quite all right, and do not worry your head

over me," Jeanne replied. "I know a charming gentleman in Monte Carlo who will welcome me, and as soon as I arrive I will find someone to give me dinner tonight."

"I am quite sure there will be no difficulty about that!" the Marquis remarked.

He put his arm through hers and walked with her through the beautifully furnished Sitting-Room into the pillared hall.

His carriage drawn by two horses was waiting outside, and Jeanne's very French lady's-maid was already seated with her back to the horses.

There were a remarkable number of trunks on top of the carriage and strapped on behind.

The Marquis assisted Jeanne onto the comfortably padded seat, and a footman covered her knees with a rug.

"Again *au revoir, Mon Cher,*" Jeanne said in the soft and provocative voice which was so much her "stock in trade."

The Marquis kissed her hand, the carriage-door was shut, and she waved as the carriage drove off.

Then, with a sigh as if of relief, the Marquis walked back the way he had come to sit down once again on the verandah, staring out to sea.

It had been a mistake, and he seldom made a mistake, to ask Jeanne to accompany him to the South of France.

He might have guessed that she would resent not having the opportunity to flaunt herself and her fabulous gowns in Monte Carlo, and to be admired on the *Promenade des Anglais* in Nice.

Instead, she found that the Marquis, whom she had known for several years before he inherited the title, wished to sit in his newly-acquired Villa eating the excellent food provided by his superlative Chef.

He wanted to have her entertain him, as she had said quite frankly, not only at night but during the day.

The Marquis had realised twenty-four hours after their arrival that he should have come alone and that Jeanne would find it incredibly dull.

As she had said to him before packing her boxes:

"As a lover *tu es magnifique!* As a conversationalist a bore!"

It had not sounded so blunt in French, but, nevertheless, as the Marquis knew, it was the truth and he had no one to blame but himself.

He had come to the South of France merely to think over what the future held for him and to escape from the festivities of the Queen's Diamond Jubilee.

What he thought of to himself as the explosion of national emotion called "New Imperialism."

As Victor Bourne—he had not used his title abroad—he had travelled to many unknown parts of the World because they interested him, and he had no wish to go home.

After the death of his elder brother, who had always been a sickly child, when he himself was seventeen his father had begun to drill into his mind the responsibilities he would inherit.

The old Marquis was a despot who ruled his family, his estate, and everybody with who he came in contact, with a rod of iron.

It was typical of the old Imperialism, Victor thought, which disliked change, and which looked on Queen Victoria as representing everything that was right and proper in those who served her.

He thought now with a slight twist of his lips that his father, like every man of his age, had every reason to be proud of the Queen.

She ruled over the largest Empire in the history of the world, comprising nearly a quarter of the earth, besides a quarter of its population.

Victor found it difficult to forget, and it amused him that the Queen herself had been "Queen Empress" for so long that some of her simpler subjects in India whom he had met on his travels considered her Divine, and slaughtered goats before her image.

He knew, however, that at this moment the crowds in the streets of London would be waiting in wild excitement for the procession to appear from Buckingham Palace.

He could guess already, he thought, what the Queen's message would be.

It would be simple and to the point:

"From my heart, I thank my people, and may God Bless them."

He was sure it would be something like that, and tomorrow would prove him right.

However, what concerned him more than the

Diamond Jubilee was the part he would be expected to play in the future.

He was apprehensive when he returned to London on receiving the news of his father's death.

The old man had always seemed as immortal as the Queen.

He had never really considered what his position would be when he had to take over not only the title, but the many duties that were expected of the Marquis of Quinbourne.

When he had been summoned by the Queen to Windsor Castle, she had made it clear that she expected him to carry on where his father had left off.

The Prime Minister, the Marquess of Salisbury, had made it even clearer.

"As soon as you have set everything in order at Quin," he said in his lofty manner, "I have a great many tasks to lay before you that will keep you a great deal in London."

He paused and then continued:

"There will be, I am afraid, no more foreign travels into the unknown which have occupied you these last years."

The Marquis was surprised, having no idea that the Prime Minister was aware of or interested in his travels.

Occasionally he was of use to the Foreign Office in reporting on and trying to explain difficulties in strange parts of the Empire.

They were usually places in which the Foreign Secretary himself had no intention of setting foot.

When he left the Prime Minister, he thought with horror of what would happen if he were to take his proper place.

First he would be a Gentleman-in-Waiting at Buckingham Palace, secondly Lord Lieutenant of the County, also there would be innumerable positions of Political and Civic importance!

It meant he would be virtually imprisoned by so many duties that the freedom he had enjoyed for the last six years would be at an end.

He had gone abroad first when he was twenty-two.

This was because he was sick of being lectured by his father, who felt that everything he did was either unbecoming to his position, or too frivolous for his consequence in the future.

His father had criticised his friends, his interests, and even his aptitude for languages.

He said there was no need for an Englishman whether he was a Statesman or a Politician, to speak anything but his own tongue.

"If those damned foreigners," he would roar, "cannot understand me, then the sooner they learn to do so, the better!"

It was the sort of attitude that Victor Bourne had not found amusing, but most irritating, especially when he heard it repeated not once, but several times a day.

He had therefore left England for Malaya without even telling his father he was going.

When he returned six months later, it was to be treated like a naughty School-boy who had "played truant" and was on the point of expulsion.

He had had to listen to his father for three months, until once again he set off on his own, finding it a delight to cease being found fault with.

Even a life of danger at the hands of savage tribesmen, cannibals, and African warriors seemed infinitely preferable to the formality and pomposity of life at Quin.

When he returned for the second time, it was not only his father who had lectured him, but many other members of the family.

The Marquis of Quinbourne had not only what seemed an abnormal number of Bourne relations, but was also connected with many other aristocratic families.

Victor was the "black sheep" and was set on, he told himself, by a pack of ravaging wolves.

The men told him he was not being particularly sporting in his treatment of his father.

The women were kinder because he was so attractive and good-looking.

He was told that the only way he could find favour was to be married and settle down.

A number of débutantes were produced for him by his grandmother, his aunts, his cousins.

There were dinner-parties, Balls, Receptions, and house-parties at which inevitably he was paired off with some gauche, rather shy young woman.

He was then informed that she would make him an extremely suitable and acceptable wife.

It was inevitable that he took himself off abroad as quickly as possible.

This time he quarrelled with his father to the point where he was told that, unless he behaved himself, he need not come back.

He had, in fact, in the years that followed, twice returned unexpectedly for a few days at Christmas and once in the Summer.

He had felt irresistibly drawn by the beauties of Quin itself, if not by the people living in it.

There were always the same old arguments, the same old criticisms which had driven him away again.

Finally he came home because his father was dead and he was now, when he least expected it, the Marquis of Quinbourne.

He had arrived only just before the Funeral, to find the great house packed with relations.

All of them, he thought somewhat cynically, fawned upon him because he was now the head of the family.

They did not lecture him, they pleaded with him.

"Dearest Victor, I know you will help me over this. Your father has always been so kind, I am sure you will help me, as he has done."

"I want your advice..." "I want your attention..." "I want you to listen..."

It seemed to him that a thousand voices were

echoing in his ears, cramming his mind with small domestic and financial troubles.

They were very different from the problems with which he had been faced on his travels.

Quite a number of them could be quite easily dealt with with the assistance of his secretary, who had been employed by his father for over ten years and knew far more, not only about the estate, but also about the Bourne Family, than he did.

When the Funeral was over, he went from Quin to stay at Bourne House in Park Lane.

He was aware that it was not only his family who looked upon him as a cornucopia.

The Queen, the Prime Minister, the Secretary for Foreign Affairs, and inevitably a number of his friends he found at Whites looked upon him in the same way.

It was all too much, too overwhelming and, he thought cynically, positively humiliating.

That people should want to ingratiate themselves with him simply because he was rich and socially important was an unpleasant contrast to the life he had lived abroad.

There, a man was accepted for himself, and possessions were of secondary importance.

Finally, as he opened one letter after another from Statesmen, from the Prime Minister downwards, demanding his attention, he had run away.

It was something he had done so often before that it presented no particular difficulty to him.

He had left London without telling anyone except his seretary where he was going.

He stopped in Paris to pick up Jeanne Beauvais and with her travelled to his father's Villa near Eze, where he wanted to think about the future.

On one thing he was absolutely determined—that he would not marry.

"*I particularly want you to dine with me on Wednesday,*" his aunt, the Duchess of Weybridge, had written to him.

"*I have a charming girl for you to meet—the daughter of the Duke of Hull. I know she would suit you admirably and would make a perfect Chatelaine for Quin. She speaks French and Italian very prettily, and I feel you will have, with your interest in languages, a bond in common.*"

The Marquis had thrown back his head and laughed as he had read the letter.

He wondered what the Duchess would say if he told her he would only marry a girl who could speak Japanese, Russian, and Afrikaans.

Then he told himself he was being unkind.

It would be even more cruel to raise the young woman's hopes by agreeing to meet her at dinner, when she would certainly have been encouraged to look on him as her future husband.

He was so appalled at the feeling he was being pressured, pursued, pushed almost by force into matrimony, that he had sought out Jeanne as if he thought she could protect him.

He was fortunate in finding that at that moment

there was nobody occupying any exclusive position in her life.

Because they had had some very amusing times together in the past, she accepted eagerly his suggestion that she should come with him to the *Côte d'Azur*.

It had never struck him that she would find it exceedingly dull if they did not spend most of the daytime in the Casino.

Or that she would want to be seen by the fashionable world who always travelled to Monte Carlo at this time of the year and made it the most entrancing and expensive playground in Europe.

What the Marquis had not taken into account was that he was in mourning for his father.

It would be considered exceedingly heartless to accept invitations to dinner parties and other social functions for at least another two or three months.

There would certainly be raised eyebrows in the *salle privée* if he were to appear there with a notorious and attractive French *cocotte*.

He realised that Jeanne was exceedingly bored unless he was making love to her.

In fact, what he had not realised before, she had little to say beyond witty remarks that inevitably concerned *l'amour*, or paying him compliments for his expertise in the same subject.

"I have made a mistake," the Marquis told himself.

He told Jeanne that he would not be in the least offended if she left him to stay in Monte

Carlo, where he was sure she would not be alone for more than twenty-four hours.

Now he was alone and once again he was wondering what he should do.

He knew that if he behaved with propriety, he should return to England.

He should take up the duties that were waiting for him, and try to make them as interesting as the discovery of a long-forgotten Temple in the centre of a jungle.

He had spent many years exploring, being the first white man to sail up an uncharted river, discovering a tribe that was not previously known to other explorers.

On so many occasions he had avoided death only by inches, that the idea of what was called "settling down" appalled him.

He had the uncomfortable feeling that never again would people speak to him naturally.

They would always adopt the respectful attitude that his father had commanded not only because of his title, but because he had an appreciation of his own consequence.

"I want to be myself," he said to the sunshine glinting on the sea.

Then it was as if a voice added:

"I also want to be loved for myself."

There had been many women in his life, many of them like Jeanne, because it was possible to pay them and leave without tears and recriminations.

There had been others of various foreign nationalities who he knew had found him irresistibly attractive, but had been for him just a passing fancy, and once he had left them, he had never thought of them again.

There had never been any question of his meeting a woman whom he wished to have permanently in his life and who would not restrict him on his travels, which were often uncomfortable, exhausting, and dangerous.

"What shall I do?" he asked the scene in front of him, feeling as if the sea itself would give him an answer, or that the gulls circling overhead could decide the issue.

Down in the harbour there was his father's yacht, which he had used for only a few weeks of each year, but which was kept in readiness just in case it should be wanted.

'How rich men live!' the Marquis thought with a smile.

He remembered how often he had been short of money because his father had stopped his allowance.

It meant he had to take lodgings that were cheap and often verminous, and sail in boats that were leaking.

On one occasion, he had to resort to a tent in the desert which he had shared with a very scruffy Arab.

He now had at least six houses of which he was the owner, horses which filled several large stables, and he was tempted before he left England into buying a motorcar.

"In the circumstances, how can I complain?" the Marquis asked aloud.

He thought of Quin and all it entailed, and the Prime Minister and the Queen sitting like large spiders waiting to catch him in their webs.

He looked towards the horizon, where the sea met the sky, and knew what he wanted to do.

There was no question of which route he should take.

But at the moment, mockingly, he thought, the best way to make his decision was to toss a coin into the air and let that make his mind up for him.

"Shall I go North or South?" he asked the Fates.

It was the same way he had asked them when he was lost in the forests or in a desert and knew that to make the wrong decision might easily result in his leaving his bones where he fell.

It was actually because the idea amused him that he had put his hand into his pocket, seeking a coin, when a respectful voice behind him said in French:

"Pardon, Milord, but there is someone to see you."

"Who is it?" the Marquis asked.

It flashed through his mind that one of his friends or acquaintances had learned that he was at the Villa and had driven out from Monte Carlo to see him.

"It is a Monsieur Kirkpatrick who is at the door," the servant answered.

The Marquis wrinkled his brow.

He could not think of anyone of that name, but after a moment, more because of curiosity than anything else, he said:

"Show him in."

As the servant left, he thought perhaps he had made a mistake.

If the man was collecting for charity and he gave him a donation, it would very likely lead to many other appeals to his generosity.

He had no intention of staying here long or becoming embroiled in local affairs in which he was not particularly interested.

But before he could properly formulate what he was feeling, a man came through the window which opened onto the verandah.

As the Marquis rose slowly from the chair in which he had been sitting, he saw he was not alone, but was accompanied by a young women.

The newcomer held out his hand.

"It is very kind of you to see me, My Lord, and I have called because I have something of great import to tell you, something which I feel you will find exciting as well as intriguing."

The Marquis was surprised.

Then because he was used to sizing up men of every type and nationality, he took in every detailof his caller's appearance.

He was tall, very slim, good-looking, obviously educated, and what one would call a "gentleman."

At the same time, the Marquis was perceptively aware that he was an Adventurer.

He was not certain quite how he knew this, but

perhaps it was something in the man's manner: a slight eccentricity of dress, or perhaps the boldness of his eyes.

The Marquis had met many adventurers in his travels and was sure even before his caller spoke again that that was what he was.

"My name is Michael Kirkpatrick," he said, "and may I present my daughter Sabra?"

The Marquis had hardly noticed that the young woman had followed Michael Kirkpatrick onto the verandah.

She was small and slim and was wearing a large-brimmed hat, very plain and trimmed with only a green ribbon.

Beneath it her face was in shadow, and she also wore tinted spectacles which made her seem not only anonymous, but somehow dowdy and unimportant.

He glanced at her, then back again at her father.

Without waiting to be asked, Michael Kirkpatrick sat down comfortably in one of the armchairs and it was quite obvious he was hoping for some refreshment.

"May I offer you a drink?" the Marquis asked automatically, as if he were compelled to do so.

"That is exceedingly kind of you, and what I was hoping you would say. We have walked up from the Lower Corniche and I found it extremely heating at this time of the day."

It was not so much what he said, but the way he said it that made the Marquis laugh.

The servant who had announced the guests was waiting in the doorway and the Marquis said almost as if Kirkpatrick were willing him to do so:

"Bring a bottle of champagne."

"That is even kinder of you!" Michael Kirkpatrick said with a smile.

There was something ingenuous and at the same time fascinating about him that made the Marquis even surer that he was an Adventurer.

He had obviously walked to the Villa, which was quite a considerable distance, because he could afford no means of conveyance.

"I am interested in what you have to tell me," the Marquis prompted.

"I have heard about you in many parts of the world . . ." Michael Kirkpatrick began.

The Marquis raised his eyebrows and Kirkpatrick continued.

"I see you doubt me, but we were in Singapore just after you left, and last year someone was talking about you in Shepherds Hotel in Cairo."

The Marquis laughed.

"I hope what they said was complimentary!"

"Very, as it happens."

The Marquis would have asked further questions, but at that moment the servant returned with the champagne which he had obviously had ready.

He opened the bottle, filled the glassses, and offered them round, and then replaced the bottle in the wine-cooler before he retired.

Michael Kirkpatrick raised his glass.

"Your health, My Lord!"

"Thank you."

The Marquis noticed that Sabra, and he thought it a very unusual name, took only a sip of the champagne before she set it down.

Then she looked, as he had, out at the horizon and seemed completely uninterested in what was being said.

It struck the Marquis as being somewhat strange.

But he was aware of her because she seemed different and certainly uninterested in him as a man.

"What I came to ask you," Michael Kirkpatrick began after he had drunk from his glass of champagne, "is whether you are interested in finding a treasure that would not only be a triumph for you, but a delight to every historian."

"I can hardly answer that question," the Marquis said a little coldly, "until you tell me what the treasure consists of and where you think it can be found."

He felt as he spoke that he had been quite right in thinking that Kirkpatrick was an Adventurer.

At the same time, he found it impossible not to rather like the man.

He was undoubtedly well-bred, as most Adventurers were not, and he had that magnetic charm which made an Adventurer accepted by people who would otherwise have had nothing to do with him.

They were like gamblers who staked their last penny on the turn of a card.

Except, where Adventurers were concerned, they gambled not with money but with people, using them in strange ways, and for strange purposes, as the Marquis had discovered.

They did not usually ask for cash that they could put in their pockets, but rather they would want some plan, some project financed.

Several Adventurers had attached themselves to the Marquis to ask only that he provide a roof over their heads and enough food to keep them alive.

He had the idea that Kirkpatrick was one of these, yet he was quite unlike any of the parasites with whom he had been involved in the past.

"It has come to my knowledge," Kirkpatrick was saying, "that in the country which we now call Tunisia, an extremely rich Roman General was once robbed not only of his money but also of his wife's jewellery."

The Marquis smiled to himself.

He thought this sounded a very unlikely story and was quite certain Kirkpatrick had invented it.

"What I have learned," Michael Kirkpatrick went on, "is that having stolen from the General what he had previously extorted from the wretched people over whom he ruled, the robbers buried the treasure not far from the amphitheatre at El Djem and beneath a wayside Temple, which is now in ruins."

He paused to see if the Marquis was listening,

then, sipping a little more champagne from his glass, he went on:

"Two of the thieves were captured, but even under torture they would not reveal where the treasure was hidden."

He paused again before he went on:

"Shortly after, they were put to death, but before further enquiries could be made, the Roman rule in North Africa began to collapse and the lost treasure was forgotten."

"How do you know all this?" the Marquis enquired.

"I was told it by a man who said the oldest inhabitants in that part of Tunisia talked about it openly, and the story had been handed down from generation to generation by word of mouth."

"And you really believe after all this time that you and I could find this treasure that has been hidden for so long?" the Marquis asked sarcastically.

Michael Kirkpatrick did not speak for a moment. Then he said:

"I know exactly what you are feeling. It is what I would feel myself, My Lord, if I were told such a 'cock and bull' story by somebody like me!"

The Marquis laughed.

The man was certainly disarming, and he liked the way his eyes twinkled when he said such unexpected things.

"I would have doubted it too," Michael Kirkpatrick was saying, "if I had not had the opportunity to buy this."

22

He put his hand into his pocket as he spoke and brought out a gold coin which he handed to the Marquis.

The Marquis, who was a connoisseur of coins, recognised it at once as a coin which had been struck by the Romans when they were in Tunisia and used over the whole area.

It was, in fact, in excellent condition, and he was sure the British Museum and certainly the antiquarian authorities in Rome would, if it were for sale, be prepared to buy it.

"The man who sold me this coin," Michael Kirkpatrick explained, "was hounded out of Tunisia a month or so ago for stealing and desecrating property which the authorities thought should be preserved."

"You mean—he found the treasure?"

"He found where he thought it was hidden and had time to excavate only this, and several other coins like it."

He hesitated, and after making sure the Marquis was listening intently, continued:

"Unfortunately, he foolishly robbed a living victim, was caught, taken to Tunis, convicted of theft, and served two years in gaol before, because he is an Englishman, he was deported from the country."

"Which means he will never have a chance to go back!" the Marquis remarked.

"If he enters Tunisia again, he will be imprisoned for life, or else shot! They are allergic to thieves of his sort!"

Michael Kirkpatrick laughed before he added:

"What is his loss might be our gain. For a comparatively small sun, because he is hard up, he is prepared to explain exactly where the treasure is and even draw a map of the place."

He paused and lowered his voice.

"Unfortunately, I am not in a financial position to explore this on my own, nor would I have sufficient standing with the authorities. I need a partner, and your reputation as an explorer, My Lord, stands, as I have already said, very high."

"I think you flatter me!" the Marquis said dryly.

At the same time, he knew he was interested and even a little excited by what Michael Kirkpatrick had to tell him.

It was possible! Of course it was possible!

Although it was much more likely that the man in question, having got hold of a few Roman coins, was determined to make the most of a tale of undiscovered buried treasure and obtain a great deal more money than it was worth.

As he looked at the coin, which he knew was genuine, it seemed to him extraordinary that it was in such good condition.

Any coin that had been knocking about for so many centuries passing from one hand to another would certainly have lost its sharpness and become worn.

There was a pause before the Marquis asked:

"Do you really think you can trust this man?"

Michael Kirkpatrick made a very eloquent gesture with both his hands.

"How can you be certain you can trust anyone any more than you can trust me? The man appears genuine and I would have brought him to see you, but if once he was aware of your interest, the price would undoubtedly go up!"

The Marquis looked down again at the coin in his hand.

Always when he examined something old and previous, it seemed to him as if he felt certain vibrations emanating from it, which he could not explain.

But his perception told him clearly that it happened only if what he touched was completely and absolutely genuine.

He was sure he could feel this now, then he almost doubted his own instinct.

"And what does your daughter think about this?" he asked, more to play for time than because he was interested in the girl, who was paying no attention either to him or to her father.

For a moment Sabra did not move.

Then she turned her eyes slowly in his direction, aware as she did so that both men were waiting for an answer.

It was impossible to know what she was thinking or feeling behind the tinted glasses under the shadow of her hat.

Then she said slowly and distinctly in a soft, musical voice:

"If you are wise, My Lord, you will have nothing to do with it!"

chapter two

BECAUSE it was no less than he had expected, the Marquis was not surprised to find his new friends staying for luncheon.

Later they stayed for dinner, and finally installed themselves in two of his comfortable bedrooms for the night.

What he found amusing was that Kirkpatrick made no pretence of not trying to sponge on him.

"Your wine and food are delicious," he had said at dinner, "and it only makes me regret that we must leave earlier than is usual because we must find somewhere to sleep."

The Marquis had thought when he was dressing for dinner that this was likely to occur, and he merely said without prevarication:

"I hope you will be comfortable in the rooms in which you changed before dinner."

Kirkpatrick had lain back in his chair and laughed.

"If you saw where we stayed last night, you would know that what you are offering us is as welcome as the open gates of Paradise!"

The way he spoke made the Marquis laugh and later, very much later, when they went to bed, he thought the whole evening had been one of laughter.

He knew that Kirkpatrick had laid himself out to be amusing, but all the same his conversation was genuinely interesting and informative.

There was no doubt that he had lived a strange, roaming life on a different plane from that which the Marquis had lived, accumulating a great deal of knowledge as he did so.

The Marquis was able to talk to him of places which most people had never seen or even knew existed: of Oriental religions, many of which were erotic and sensuous or else extremely cruel.

He found that Kirkpatrick not only knew as much as he did but sometimes a great deal more.

It was only when he was lying in bed thinking it over that he remembered that they had completely ignored Sabra.

She had appeared to be listening to what they were saying, but he was not sure.

The only time he was conscious of her was when they returned to the Sitting-Room to find her examining a collection of snuff-boxes which his father had added to over the years.

It just flashed through his mind that she might be stealing them.

Then, as she put one down with a little sigh, he knew from the way her fingers moved that she was appreciating their beauty and the craftsmanship that had gone into making them.

He had been about to talk to her, when Kirkpatrick had said something amusing and once again he was laughing and Sabra was forgotten.

Now the Marquis thought it must be a very strange life for a girl.

He wondered, as her father was so flamboyant and theatrical in both his appearance and his behaviour, how she contrived to be so unobtrusive.

Perhaps the dark glasses which she did not discard during the evening somehow made her anonymous.

The Marquis was aware that when Kirkpatrick had changed into evening-clothes, they were well worn and somewhat thread-bare at the seams but had come originally from a West End Tailor.

Sabra's simple gown was obviously home-made.

He realised, because he was experienced in such matters, that she had made it of lace because lace did not crease while travelling.

Although the material was cheap, it revealed the soft curves of Sabra's body, and he thought that, while she was too thin, she was also very much a woman.

She did not stay with them long after dinner

while they talked at the fireside because it was cold in the evening when the winds blew in from the snow-clad Alps that were not very far away.

After only a short while Sabra had risen to her feet to say:

"I am going to bed, Papa."

"Quite right, my dear. I know you will sleep far better tonight than you did last night with barking dogs keeping us awake and drunkards coming home in the early hours of the morning!"

She did not reply, but the Marquis found he could read her thoughts.

She was thinking that her father was over-emphasizing their poverty so that he could appeal to the Marquis for charity, which he was sure anyway was what Kirkpatrick intended.

Sabra moved towards the door and he had to hurry to be there to open it for her.

As he did so, he noticed in the light of the chandelier that her hair was a very strange colour.

He had never thought of it before for the simple reason that she had effaced herself so completely when he was talking to her father that he had forgotten she even existed.

Now he was aware that her hair was the colour of Simonetta's which Botticelli had used in several of his unforgettable pictures.

It was a colour that no one had ever been able to reproduce artificially. A great many hairdressers of many nationalities had tried but always failed.

But the Marquis knew without being told that

Sabra's hair was completely natural and he wondered vaguely how long it was.

With a quick "goodnight" she slipped through the Sitting-Room door, across the hall, and was moving up the stairs with a speed which told him she wished to get away and had no desire to talk to him.

The Marquis was not a conceited man, but he was well aware that wherever he went, women looked at him with admiration.

Also, rather than being eager to leave him, they usually made it difficult for him to extract himself from their company.

He shut the Sitting-Room door and returned to the hearth-rug, where he found Kirkpatrick so entertaining that they talked until it was nearly two o'clock in the morning.

Then, as they were going up to bed, Kirkpatrick said casually:

"You have not told me yet whether you intend to accompany me to Tunisia. I shall be very disappointed if I have to find somebody else."

"You are determined to go?" the Marquis asked.

"How could I resist such a challenge?" Kirkpatrick asked. "And I cannot believe it is not something that you do not find intriguing."

It was as if he were hypnotising him, the Marquis thought a little dryly.

Because the man needed him, and because he himself had no particular desire to return to England, he said as they reached Kirkpatrick's door:

31

"I will certainly consider it, and I will give you my answer at breakfast-time."

"I shall keep my fingers crossed," Kirkpatrick replied, "and as there is a new moon, I shall bow to it seven times, which I am told in Monte Carlo is an unbeatable charm!"

They both laughed and, as he turned away, the Marquis thought that Kirkpatrick would still be laughing because he had found a "mug" to finance his fantasy.

He told himself as he got into bed that he did not believe for one moment that the treasure was there, and he was sure that Kirkpatrick had invented the whole story just to arouse his interest.

The real object was to ensure that the Adventurer and his daughter would have their meals paid for and have no living expenses for at least the next two months.

The Marquis wondered whether, if he asked Kirkpatrick how much money he actually possessed at the moment, he would tell him the truth, which he was sure would be literally a few shillings.

He had noticed the way both father and daughter ate the excellent food that was provided at dinner.

Not that they gobbled!

What told him they were hungry and had eaten very sparsely for days, perhaps longer, was the fact that they ate slowly, savouring every morsel.

Also the Marquis knew from experience that it

was difficult to eat a great deal after having had hardly enough to keep alive.

Kirkpatrick had eaten everything that had been put in front of him and had shown he was very knowledgeable about wine, guessing with surprising accuracy the year the wine he was drinking had been bottled.

This made the Marquis realise that he had at one time in his life been wealthy enough to buy anything he wanted.

If there was one thing the Marquis really enjoyed, it was a mystery, a puzzle he had to unravel, or a secret he had to discover.

It was what he had sought in his travels and what he liked to find in people.

One of the reasons that he felt depressed about the future was that everybody he had met at Quin, and most of those with whom he had conversed in London, had been entirely predictable in everything they said.

He was aware as soon as he met them that to his sharp and acute perception they were like an open book.

It was what he had felt, too, when he was alone with Jeanne for far longer than he had ever been at any other time.

Before, when they were not making love, they had been in some exotic place of amusement, or attending parties where the women were of the same profession as herself.

Or else they had been eating in Restaurants where there was music from an Orchestra, the chatter of the other diners, and the light, witty conversation at which the French excelled.

But alone in the quietness of the Villa he had found he knew everything that Jeanne was going to say before she even parted her red lips.

Her moods, which were sometimes perverse, sometimes provocative or flirtatious, were equally predicable, and he discovered that if she had found him a bore, so had he found her.

When he thought it over, he found that this evening had been delightful because it had stimulated his brain.

At the same time, it aroused in him a curiosity to know more about Kirkpatrick.

That the man was a gentleman he had known as soon as they met, but he was also an Adventurer.

Yet he was a man of immense charm, with a fund of laughter that was unlike anything the Marquis had ever encountered previously.

He was also slightly curious about Sabra.

It seemed out of character that she should be so quiet and unobtrusive.

In fact, he thought somewhat cynically that if Kirkpatrick had a pretty daughter, it was only to be expected that he would use her to attract rich men whose money he needed to finance his fantasies.

Before the Marquis fell asleep, he had made up his mind.

Treasure or no treasure, he would go to Tunisia.

At least it would be better than returning to

England, where the pack of ravaging wolves would be waiting to tear him to pieces.

The Marquis rose early, which was something he had done for many years, and was surprised when he walked out onto the verandah where he had breakfast to find Sabra standing looking out to sea.

She was not wearing her hat, and the morning sun on her strangely coloured hair made the Marquis look at her more closely.

She still had on the disfiguring glasses that seemed too large for her small face, and now he was aware that she had a straight little aristocratic nose and her lips were perfectly curved.

She was wearing, however, the same gown she had worn yesterday which had something casual yet artistic about it.

It made him think she had deliberately copied the artists, who were the only people in the South of France who were not fashionable or expensively dressed.

Sabra did not turn her head as the Marquis came into the verandah, but he had the idea that she was aware of him so that she stiffened a little as if he intruded on her thoughts.

"Good morning!" he said with deliberate casualness.

Instead of joining her at the balustrade, he walked to the breakfast-table and sat down, knowing the servants would immediately bring out the food.

Sabra did not move, and after a moment, because it annoyed him that she should not be more attentive to him, he said:

"I hope you will join me, unless you have already had your breakfast?"

A little reluctantly it seemed, she turned from her contemplation of the view and walked slowly towards the table.

She had a grace of movement despite the casualness of her clothes, and she sat down at the other end of the table as far from the Marquis as possible.

"I hope you slept well," he said as if he would force her to speak to him.

"Very well, thank you. Your Villa is very comfortable."

"I thought you would find it so, especially after your father had described so eloquently the discomforts of your lodgings of the previous night."

If he was attempting to needle her into saying more, he was unsuccessful.

The servants brought coffee, hot croissants in a wicker basket covered with a linen napkin, and for the Marquis a dish of eggs and bacon.

The Marquis looked towards Sabra, then he remarked:

"I see you like the French way of having a light *petit déjeuner*, but I am sure your father will prefer, as I do, the English habit of starting the day with something substantial."

Sabra did not reply, and after a moment the Marquis said:

"Am I not right?"

"Papa expends so much energy in one way or another," Sabra replied, "that he obviously needs sustenance."

She spoke mockingly, almost as if she found it a nuisance that the Marquis must talk to her.

He felt piqued at her behaviour simply because he could not find an explanation for it.

"Tell me," he said after a moment, "why do you think the expedition which interests your father so much and which he is so keen we should undertake is a mistake?"

He was determined to make her answer him, and when she hesitated, he said impatiently:

"I want you to tell me the truth and not placate me with something which you think I want to hear."

"I have told you the truth," Sabra said. "I think it is a waste of your time."

"Are you thinking of me, or of yourself?"

"You asked me a question and I have answered it!"

The way she spoke told the Marquis she was resenting his questioning her, but because he was determined to make her speak, he said:

"I would like you to elaborate a little more on the subject. I gather you suspect the treasure of which your father has heard is non-existent."

He paused, but she did not speak.

"In which case, we shall have had our journey for nothing. But it might be enjoyable to see Tunisia, unless you have been there already?"

Again there was no reply, and after a moment the Marquis said:

"I asked you a question, and I consider it very rude of you not to answer me!"

As he spoke sharply, he realised that it was the first time he had perturbed her, and he saw the colour rise in her cheeks as she said:

"I . . . apologise. I did not mean to be . . . rude, but I thought you would not be . . . interested in my opinions and there was therefore . . . no point in saying what I . . . thought."

"If I were not interested in what you thought," the Marquis replied, "I would not have questioned you in the first place!"

For a moment he thought she was going to continue to be unresponsive, then she said in a different tone:

"Why do you . . . wish to take any . . . notice of us? We are . . . strangers to you . . . and you live in a very different . . . world from ours."

Now there was a note in her voice which told the Marquis that she was not only resenting what was happening, but was perturbed that he should be involved with them.

"In answer to your question," he said, "I have travelled a great deal, and when your father and you arrived here, I was in fact considering whether I should set off alone."

He stopped to look at her.

"I did not know whether to travel South or go back to England, where a great many unpleasant responsibilities are waiting for me."

"And now you have made up your mind?"

"I told your father I would give him my answer this morning at breakfast, but he is obviously in no particular hurry to hear it."

Sabra looked towards the open window as if she thought her father might suddenly materialise, then she said in a soft voice:

"Papa is tired. He has been very worried lately, so I think he is enjoying a comfortable bed and feeling there is no reason for him to hurry."

It was obvious from the way she spoke that she was fond of her father, and the Marquis thought that at least she had one human trait about her, but he was not sure if she had any other.

"And yet," he said after a moment, "knowing that your father would enjoy travelling with me and that you would both be more comfortable than if your went alone, you are tying to prevent me from helping him to do what he wishes."

"No one could . . . prevent Papa from doing anything he really wants!" Sabra said quickly. "What I am against is that you should agree to . . . undertake this . . . trip when you are obviously wanted . . . in England."

Now the Marquis stared at her in surprise.

He found it annoying that because of her glasses he could not read the expression on her face.

"What do you mean—I am wanted in England? What do you know about me?"

She turned her head and looked away towards the sunshine in the garden.

The bougainvillaea and the climbing pink geraniums were making brilliant patches of colour just below them, as were the hibiscus blossoms.

There was silence save for the buzzing of the bees and the fluttering wings of a bird.

Because they were sitting very still, it alighted on the blaustrade of the verandah to look with sharp, greedy little eyes at the breakfast-table.

The Marquis suddenly found himself incensed.

"For Heaven's sake, girl," he said, "stop playing at being mysterious and answer my questions! What did you know about me before you came here last night?"

"Now I have . . . made you . . . angry," Sabra said in a very small voice, "and that would not . . . please Papa. I am . . . sorry for what I said. It was a . . . mistake."

"It was not a mistake," the Marquis replied. "I asked for your opinion, and I am immensely interested to know what you have heard about me and why you should think that I am wanted in England."

Sabra smiled, and as it was the first time she had done so, the Marquis thought that despite her glasses it made her look attractive.

"Papa is English," she said softly, "and, despite everything, often homesick for his own country."

She paused before continuing:

"When he can afford it, he buys English newspapers, but they are also obtainable in some Libraries, or . . . thrown away from . . . rich hotels."

"Are you telling me," the Marquis said after a moment, "that you rifle through the dustbins?"

Sabra made a little gesture with her hands that was apologetic.

"When it is . . . necessary."

"And so you have read about me in the newspapers!" he insisted.

"We read that you had . . . arrived, that you are here at this . . . Villa, that your father had . . . recently died, and you had been to Windsor Castle to see . . . the Queen."

"I am honoured that you find me so interesting!" the Marquis said sarcastically. "That, of course, is what made your father realise that I could be useful to him."

He felt as he spoke that he was putting it rather bluntly, and Sabra looked down before she said in the same small voice that she had used before:

"I am sorry . . . I should not have said . . . anything to . . . upset you."

"You have not upset me," the Marquis contradicted. "You, or rather your father, have made up my mind that I will not return to England for the moment but will visit Tunisia or any other part of the world which I find interesting."

Sabra opened her lips to speak, then shut them again.

"Why do you not say what you are thinking?" the Marquis asked. "That it is my *duty* to do what is expected of me, both for my Queen and for my country."

"I did not . . . say that!"

"But you were thinking it."

"You should not . . . read my . . . thoughts!"

"Why not? Unless you have something to hide."

"My thoughts are my own, and they are . . . private and . . . secret."

"Not always to me!" the Marquis boasted.

"You mean . . . you can read my thoughts . . . and other people's?"

"I mean that over the years I have found it very useful to know what a man is thinking before he acts. It has undoubtedly saved my life on various occasions."

"That is excusable, but I think it is an . . . intrusion that you use your perception in that way unless . . . it is absolutely . . . necessary."

"So you know that a perception becomes more and more acute the more it is used."

She did not reply, and after a moment he said:

"I think—unless I am mistaken—that it is what you do yourself."

"Now you are guessing," Sabra said, "or are you once again . . . reading my . . . thoughts?"

"Whichever it is, the result is the same," the Marquis replied. "If you are perceptive, then it is impossible for you not to be aware of things that people are unwilling to tell you in words, and often have no wish for you to know."

There was silence until Sabra said defiantly:

"I have never met . . . anyone who could read my thoughts before . . . and it is . . . something I do not . . . like!"

She got up from the table as she spoke and, walking to the centre of the verandah, went down the steps which led into the garden.

The Marquis could see her golden head moving amongst the trees until she walked into their shadow and he could see her no longer.

He sat back in his chair and thought it was an extraordinary conversation to have had with anyone.

Especially with a young woman who obviously had no liking for him and who, despite his perception, did not fit into any category of women he had met in the past.

It was then, as he was thinking about Sabra and how strange she was, that her father came onto the verandah.

He was looking extremely Bohemian with a red handkerchief tied round his neck instead of a tie and without a coat to cover his white shirt.

Yet within two seconds of his arrival the Marquis found himself laughing and it was impossible after that to be serious about anything.

But the journey which they were to take together required, the Marquis was sure, a considerable amount of hard planning if things were to be as easy and comfortable as he intended.

Later in the day the Marquis drove with Kirkpatrick in an open carriage to the Quay and boarded his yacht which was anchored in the harbour.

It had been refurbished and improved in various ways only two years before the late Marquis had died, and it was obviously a vast expense to keep when it was so seldom used.

Now the Marquis thought it would conveniently carry them to Tunisia.

He was aware that the Captain was delighted at the thought that his new master wished to avail himself of the yacht which actually had not been used for a year.

Kirkpatrick was also full of suggestions as to what they would want in the way of clothing, and so having spent a considerable sum of money in the shops in Nice, they returned to the Villa.

It did not surprise the Marquis that Kirkpatrick had said his daughter had no wish to accompany them and would prefer to stay quietly in the garden.

He had a feeling, although it seemed unreasonable, that he had somehow frightened her at breakfast, and he thought that she was very silent at luncheon.

She was deliberately "closing in" on herself, as if to prevent him from intruding on her.

He could not explain why he knew it, but he knew she was doing so just as the Fakirs he had seen in India.

They went into a trance so that they were not only completely oblivious to what was happening around them, but if pricked with a pin, they felt no pain.

It was impossible to waken them until they were ready to be awakened, and in the same way other people could withdraw into themselves.

He was sure this was what Sabra was doing, and he could not understand why it should be from him.

He was so used to women vibrating towards him and showing they were genuinely attracted by him physically that he thought he must be mistaken.

Yet again, when they were at luncheon and her father was making him laugh, the Marquis thought it was just as if Sabra were no longer there.

It was almost as if he had to put out his hand to touch her to be sure she was not just an illusion and was actually made of flesh and blood.

Then he told himself he was being ridiculous, and it was only because the girl surprisingly was not interested in him as a man that he was taking any notice of her at all.

Only when he and Kirkpatrick were on their own did he say:

"I think it wise of your daughter to rest while she has the opportunity. Surely it is a rather strange life for anyone so young?"

"My dear fellow, I have no alternative," Kirkpatrick replied. "Her mother, whom I loved very dearly, is dead and I have no wish to live in England."

He paused a moment before he went on:

"Anyway, I find the world an entrancing place and I would not wish for any other life. But there is no one with whom I could have left Sabra."

"It is hardly a proper existence for a girl!" the Marquis remarked.

"It is exciting, and there is always something new," Kirkpatrick parried.

The Marquis could hardly argue with this when he was aware it was what he himself was seeking.

He knew he was running away from the predicatable and everything that was secure for an adventure which he was sure was destined to end in disappointment.

Then he remembered that somebody had once said to him:

"It is not what you achieve which counts. It is the effort you make in doing it which is important."

"That is what I am doing now," he excused himself, and tried not to remember that Sabra had said he was wanted in England.

Kirkpatrick was obviously elated that the Marquis had agreed that they would search for the hidden treasure together.

"I am looking forward to seeing Tunisia," he said, "although I am told that the Roman remains there are not as fine as those in Algeria. But the people are more friendly and because it is also under French domination the food is just as good!"

"That is at least something in its favour!" the Marquis replied dryly.

He was thinking of the unpalatable meals he had been offered in various parts of the world.

It was often easier to go hungry then to abuse one's palate and one's stomach with food that would be refused by any self-respecting animal.

He therefore ordered the Captain of the yacht

to take aboard the best food available and it could be very good indeed if the Chef was discriminating.

As there seemed to be no point in waiting, the Marquis decided to leave the next afternoon.

He thought that would give the Captain time to have everything ready.

It would also give him time to write the letters which had to be sent to England explaining that his absence would be somewhat longer than he had originally intended.

He was quite certain that his Manager at Quin and his secretary in London would see that everything carried on in the same way as it had done for years.

He had not yet visited his other properties at Newmarket, in Leicestershire, and the North, where he owned a grouse moor and a salmon river.

These places could all wait, and if anything were wrong, he would put it right on his return.

What was far more difficult was his letter to the Prime Minister, the Marquess of Salisbury, explaining that he would not for the moment be able to take up his duties at Court, and asking him to explain his absence to Her Majesty.

"Dammit!" he said to himself, suddenly putting down his pen. "Why the hell should I become embroiled in that sort of life? In the past it has never mattered to anyone except myself what I did, or where I went."

He wondered if anyone in his position had ever

relinquished the title, handed over his estates to his heir presumptive, or just disappeared without explaining why.

Then he remembered that his heir presumptive was an elderly uncle who had five daughters and no son, and after him a cousin who was middle-aged and unmarried.

This situation had been presented to him so often as a reason why he should be married, and as soon as possible, that he knew for him to abdicate his responsibilities was impossible.

Although he hated to admit it, he was very proud of Quin. He loved its beauty, its dignity, and also its history down the ages.

It was his relations whom he found suffocating, and yet in the past there had been Bournes who had served their Sovereign and their country brilliantly.

They had the unmistakable bravery and intelligence which, if his father had not quoted them so continuously, he himself would have found heroic.

'Perhaps this is my last fling,' he thought as he addressed the letters to England.

He thought of the gauche young women who had been offered to him as suitable wives, and shuddered.

How could he spend the rest of his life seeing them opposite him at breakfast and knowing before they parted their lips exactly what they were going to say?

It would be the same thing they had said yesterday, the day before, and the day before that.

"I cannot do it!" the Marquis said despairingly.

He thought the best thing he could do would be to go to Paris and find a *cocotte* like Jeanne, who would make him forget everything except the exotic pleasures of passion.

It was only a palliative, as he had already discovered, and all he wanted was to ignore what he ought to do, and do what would amuse him.

That was to allow Kirkpatrick to lead him on what he was convinced would be a "wild goose chase."

But he would undoubtedly make him laugh and that was certainly an antidote to boredom.

Sabra appeared at dinner-time wearing, the Marquis noticed, the same dress that she had worn the night before.

As she came into the Sitting-Room where he and her father were waiting for her, he realised she had not been consulted as to what she would need on the journey which lay ahead of them.

"I expect your father has told you," he said, "that we are leaving for Tunisia tomorrow afternoon."

He smiled at her and went on:

"I am sure there must be many things you will want to buy for what I gather may be an arduous expedition. We will also be staying in Tunis and perhaps in other towns as well."

He paused, but Sabra did not say anything, and after a moment he went on:

"I suggest you might like to go into Nice tomorrow morning and buy anything you require. I am of course prepared to be your Banker."

He smiled again as he finished speaking, feeling that any woman would find it an enjoyable prospect to spend quite a lot of money and it was something he could well afford.

To his surprise Sabra stiffened before she said:

"Thank you, My Lord...but I have... everything I...want."

"That is ridiculous!" her father interposed before the Marquis could reply. "Of course you want new clothes. As you told me only a few days ago, the gowns you are wearing are threadbare, and I am tired of seeing you in that tatty lace!"

"Then there is no need for you to look at me!" Sabra retorted. "As I have already said, I want nothing, and anyway, I doubt if on this expedition there will be people of any importance to criticise me."

"That is where you might be wrong!" Kirkpatrick said. "We are travelling, my dear, with a very important nobleman."

He stopped speaking a moment to look at her closely.

"Not only the Governor and the Mayor, but 'Uncle Tom Cobbleigh and All' will wish to meet him, so we must do our best not to let him down."

"One thing is quite certain," Sabra said softly, "there is no one who will be interested in meeting me, and I can either stay at home, wherever that may be, or, if you prefer, wait for you in the street outside."

"Oh, for God's sake, do not be such a little fool!" Kirkpatrick said in exasperated tones.

He did not need to elaborate either to the Marquis or to Sabra that she was being extremely obtuse and stubborn.

It certainly seemed very foolish not to accept expensive clothes when they were offered to her without any strings attached by a rich man who could well afford to pay for them.

It amused the Marquis to realise that Sabra intended to defy her father.

While he was well aware that the Adventurer was incensed by his daughter's obstinacy, Sabra, quite unabashed, was looking down into the fire unselfconscious and, he thought, relaxed.

He said nothing, and after a while Kirkpatrick said:

"You will do as our kind host suggests and go into Nice first thing tomorrow morning. Do you understand?"

"I have already told you, Papa, I have everything I want."

"And I tell you, you look a fright!" her father retorted.

"Then the best thing I can do is to buy a burnous, a yashmak, and some flip-flop slippers such as the Muslims wear. Then neither you nor anyone else will have any idea what I look like."

She spoke teasingly, but her father got up from the chair in which he was sitting and walked across the room to prevent himself, the Marquis was aware, from raging at her.

Because he had no wish to become involved in a family row, the Marquis merely filled up Kirkpatrick's glass and said:

"Let us talk about something more interesting. Do you think we shall need any books on the trip?"

He paused and smiled at Kirkpatrick.

"I noticed, and it did not surprise me, that there are no bookshelves anywhere in the yacht, and I doubt if there are any in my father's cabin."

He thought, although, of, course he could not be sure, that Sabra's eyes lit up as she said:

"I think it is very important that we should have something to read, especially if, as often happens, there is a storm in the Mediterranean and we run into a rough sea."

"I suggest you choose what books you want here," the Marquis said, "but if you do not need anything yourself, you might be kind enough to travel into Nice tomorrow morning."

The Marquis paused and smiled at her.

"There is an excellent Bookshop which will have, I am sure, the latest novels."

"Is that what you think I would like to read, or is it your choice?" Sabra asked.

She was challenging him, and the Marquis thought it was a welcome change from her habitual silence.

"Personally, I would like some books on Tunisia and, if they are obtainable, I have a *penchant* for adventure stories!"

Sabra laughed, and he thought it was a very attractive sound.

"I should have thought you had enough adventure in your own life without reading about it!"

"One never knows—one might learn a tip or two as to how to react in a difficult situation!"

"You . . . anticipate that is what we shall . . . find in . . . Tunisia?"

"One can never be sure," he answered. "Your father, who knows more about it than I do, assured me that everything is quiet, with no uprisings, and the French have everything under control."

There was a little twist to Sabra's lips, as if she thought that her father was making everything sound more attractive than it actually was, to suit his own ends.

But she said politely:

"I will try, My Lord, to find you something that you will enjoy reading, and thank you for thinking of everything which is important for your guests' comfort."

"I do my best," the Marquis said, "but my ideas are not always appreciated."

He knew as he spoke that she would understand his meaning, and she looked at him through her dark glasses before she said very quietly:

"I . . . am grateful . . . but what you have suggested is . . . something of which my . . . mother would definitely . . . disapprove."

The Marquis was surprised.

It was the first time that Sabra had ever mentioned her mother, and he had not thought that she was someone she was missing.

Then, before he could formulate his thoughts on what she had said and why she should be so vehement that he should not give her anything to wear, a servant announced dinner.

Kirkpatrick, who had been unusually silent while he controlled his temper, came from the window where he had been looking out into the darkness to join them.

chapter three

THE sea was calm and a deep Madonna blue as the yacht edged its way slowly out of the harbour and set off towards the horizon.

The Marquis had a strange feeling he was embarking on something quite new and different from anything he had done before.

He told himself it was only because he was travelling more comfortably than he had been able to do in the past, for until now he had certainly never owned a yacht.

There was no doubt that his guests were enjoying themselves.

Kirkpatrick, who had left the deck and thrown himself down into a comfortable chair in the Saloon, had already accepted a glass of champagne from the steward.

When the Marquis joined him, he held out his glass, saying:

"I am drinking to the success of our venture! Perhaps we shall find the 'Golden Fleece' or even 'The Holy Grail'!"

He gave a quick laugh.

"I cannot believe that Fate would be so unkind as to send us back empty-handed."

"It is always a good thing to be optimistic," the Marquis said.

He thought he sounded somewhat pompous as he sat down and refused a glass of champagne.

Then he opened the maps he had bought before he left.

It seemed extraordinary that so much of the Tunisian map was left blank, but he knew it was because it was not a country of great importance at the moment.

Although it might be comparatively new to tourists, its history went back thousands of years.

Phoenician colonies, he learnt, were founded a thousand years before Christ, of which Carthage became the most important settlement.

Later as "the Granary of Rome," North Africa had no equal.

Kirkpatrick watched him poring over the map with a smile before he said:

"I, too, have done my homework. As well as its major export of corn, Tunisia supplied Rome with most of its olive-oil as well as its fruit, wine, and wood. In return, Rome built Cities, roads, aqueducts, and irrigation systems."

"But today they have crumbled away into dust," the Marquis remarked, "and perhaps that is what eventually will happen to the British Empire."

Once again he was thinking of the Queen's Diamond Jubilee and how glad he was not to be taking part in it.

For the moment he wanted to immerse himself in the distant past and forget the present.

It struck him that nothing could be more appropriate than to think and dream of Tunisia at the time when it had been coveted because of its strategic position in commanding the Sicilian narrows.

Last night he had thought that Kirkpatrick was only a laughter-maker who skimmed on the surface of life and had no interest in aesthetics.

He was, therefore, surprised, when he continued to talk about Tunis, to find Kirkpatrick knew a great deal about its history, and even more about the might of the Roman Empire.

He expanded on the brilliant way in which they had conquered so much of the then known world.

As they talked, the Marquis found himself wondering if Sabra was as interested in their voyage as her father.

Despite her resistance to him personally, he could not help feeling that she would look at things in a different way from any other woman he might have invited.

He did not miss the definite eagerness of her manner as she stepped aboard *The Mermaid* and he was sure she was now standing in the bow of the yacht looking at the horizon again.

Perhaps she was dreaming that she had stepped back into the past and was visiting Carthage in its heyday.

Then he told himself it was a strange thing to be thinking about a young girl.

In all likelihood, she had no idea where Carthage was, or what it had meant in the past.

He had no opportunity, however, of asking her what her feelings were for the simple reason that she did not come into the Saloon.

When later he went on deck and onto the bridge, he could see, as he had suspected, that she had isolated herself in the bow and was looking out to sea.

It was as if her thoughts were far away in the past, or perhaps in the future, and had nothing to do with the present.

Only when it was dinner-time and she had changed once again into her lace gown did she reveal in reply to something her father said that she had, as the Marquis had thought, been thinking of Carthage.

"Does it interest you?" he asked, determined that she should answer him.

"I hate to think of it being . . . destroyed," Sabra replied.

"The Carthaginians, after being defeated and surrendering their weapons, were told they might build another City, ten miles in from the coastline," the Marquis said to test her knowledge.

"And it hurt their pride," Sabra answered. "The people rose, killed those who had counselled submission, and closing the gates, worked twenty-four hours a day to forge new weapons to replace those they had given up."

The Marquis smiled to himself, knowing he had forced her into the kind of discussion he wanted to have.

"Their effort was useless," he remembered scathingly.

"The siege dragged on for three years," Sabra said. "Women cut off their hair to make ropes, children were sacrificed to Tanit. Despite pestilence and . . . famine the . . . citizens . . . worked on."

She spoke as if it hurt her to think how much they had suffered.

"When the City fell," the Marquis said, "it burned for seventeen days, and a solemn curse was put on any person who dared to rebuild it."

"The Romans did so and eventually the . . . curse worked," Sabra retorted. "Their Empire fell into . . . ruins like the buildings they had . . . pulled down."

"So you believe in curses!" the Marquis exclaimed.

He realised as he spoke that he had stepped from the historical into the personal, and instantly Sabra was silent, as if she resented his intruding on her.

After a moment he said:

"I asked you a question, Sabra. Do you believe in curses?"

He did not notice that he had used her Christian name for the first time, and she did not seem to notice either.

She merely said reluctantly as if aware that he was waiting for her reply:

"Some . . . times."

Her father laughed.

"There are curses and curses, but where we are going, it is much easier to dispose of an unwanted rival or traveller with a snake or scorpion than with words."

"Let us hope," the Marquis said, "that we do not incur any such ill-feeling. However, if we do find your treasure, Kirkpatrick, doubtless a large number of people will be extremely envious."

"It is important they should not know about it," Kirkpatrick replied.

"That is very difficult in the East," the Marquis said, "when even the sands of the desert pass on secrets, and every bush and cactus is a listening-post."

Kirkpatrick smiled.

"I see you know your East, but I assure you we will be very careful and avoid endangering our lives unnecessarily."

"All this gets back to your daughter's curse," the Marquis said. "I have often wondered in the past if they are as effective as those who make them would have us believe."

"As Sabra said, sometimes they are, but I am sure it would be a mistake for us to be worried over curses."

He paused a moment before continuing:

"We should be thinking of the gratitude we will receive from the Historians and Antiquarians if this Roman treasure is that we hope it will be."

The yacht arrived in La Goulette, a deep-water port in the Bay of Tunis, late the following afternoon.

The City was some six miles from the sea, built at the western end of a large lagoon some three-feet deep, known as "The Little Sea."

To save going all round the lake, La Goulette was connected with the City by a canal twenty-feet deep and dredged through the lagoon.

As they approached it, the domes of the Mosques and the high, slim Minarets, and the palm trees towering over the flat-topped houses, looked very beautiful.

They were silhouetted against a wooded hill which protected the City.

The Marquis had decided it would be more convenient if they stayed in the best hotel rather than have to keep returning to the yacht.

He, therefore, had sent a message from Nice, booking them all in what he had been told was the most comfortable and most expensive hotel in the City.

He had an idea when they reached it that Sabra was impressed by the huge, cool, pillared hall, by the number of bowing servants, and the comfort of their bedrooms.

The Marquis had, of course, engaged a Sitting-

Room, so that they did not have to concern themselves with the other Visitors.

He had the feeling that Sabra was longing to be out amongst the people rather than isolated with just himself and her father.

However, she did not say so, and once again she had withdrawn into silence.

He was sure that he knew what she was thinking and was puzzled to find himself doing so.

At the same time, it was definitely intriguing, as if he had found a new game with which to amuse himself.

They ate an excellent dinner and, as usual, Sabra retired early, leaving her father and the Marquis to talk together until late into the night.

The Marquis noticed that she took with her when she retired quite a number of the books on Tunisia which had been brought ashore with their luggage.

He was quite certain she was not sleeping but poring over them in bed, and perhaps making herself more knowledgeable than he was on the history of the country.

It was Kirkpatrick rather than the Marquis who decided that they should not stay longer than was absolutely necessary in Tunis in order to avoid drawing attention to themselves.

They would get together the necessary camels, mules, and horses for their caravan to trek to El Djem, and leave as soon as they could be ready.

The Marquis found out from the hotel manager who were the most reliable people to employ.

He also insisted on inspecting himself every animal that was to accompany them before they started.

He knew well what a nuisance it was when an animal became sick, and he was also determined that they should not be overloaded as so often happened on expeditions of this sort.

There were quite a lot of extra items they had to purchase in the way of tents and fresh food which might have to last them some days if they could not replenish their stores on the way.

The Marquis noticed that Sabra was far more interested in the animals than in the food, which was scrutinised carefully by her father.

She went from camel to camel.

Although they held their heads in a disdainful manner, they seemed to appreciate the way she talked to them and patted them as she would a horse.

In his travels the Marquis had often been very grateful for camels, animals that could carry an extraordinary weight of baggage and endure more privation than any other creature.

With this in mind, he said to Sabra:

"I am sure these are young animals and will not let us down."

She looked at him and he felt that if he could see her eyes, they would be twinkling as she replied:

"When a camel finally flags, nothing can resuscitate him, which is why we have the old adage about 'the straw that broke the camel's back'!"

The Marquis laughed and said:

"That is something we must not do, and anyway, I am sure you will have no wish to be cruel."

She turned away from him as if she did not want to reply, and the Marquis wondered if she had very long eye-lashes behind her glasses.

They might be like camels' eye-lashes, which kept the sand out of their eyes, and protected them from the sun so that, unlike other animals, they never sought the shade.

Then he told himself she was a tiresome young woman and it would be far more amusing if he had brought someone sprightly and talkative on the journey.

She walked away from him and he almost wished he could leave her behind.

As if Kirkpatrick were aware that his daughter was being tiresome, he joined the Marquis and started to discuss with him the food they had bought for the journey.

He interspersed it with anecdotes so amusing and so original that once again the Marquis was laughing and Sabra was forgotten.

When they set off, the Marquis, Kirkpatrick, and Sabra were all riding the sprightly little desert horses which had a touch of Arab in them.

They rode ahead while the caravan with its colourful attendants followed behind.

The men were wearing their native hooded burnouses of camel-hair.

The women who had come to see them off were clothed in the "sifsari."

It was a length of material which covered the whole length of the body, besides the head and part of the face, a fold of it being held by the teeth.

The Marquis found it fascinating to watch the deftness with which they turned their heads to talk to each other, then swinging back again picked up the corner of the cloth in their teeth, as if it had never been dropped.

Because he had trained himself to be very observant, he knew that Sabra was watching the men, the women, and the children clad in blue or pink "fabliers."

Some of them carried satchels, others were in rags and looked pathetically hungry.

Speeded by cries of "*Marhaba*" (God go with you!) they rode out of the City and were soon on the open ground, not desert but dry sandy earth and with very little vegetation.

There were, however, trees, although not many of them, and at first the sun was very hot.

The Marquis thought it wise of Sabra to be wearing her broad-brimmed hat.

At the same time, the sunshine seemed not to make her in the least limp, rather she appeared to be pulsating with energy and feeling the same excitement that he felt himself.

There was a great deal to see and the travellers they met coming back to the City saluted them politely and wished them "*Mahdia*."

The Marquis had worked out where they should stay the first night, a place twenty miles from Tunis, where he had learned there was a passable hotel so that they would not have to erect their tents.

However, when they arrived in a large Arab village, it was far less suitable than he had anticipated and he knew he had made a mistake.

In future, he decided, it would be wiser to camp in the open rather than endure the discomforts of the rooms they were allotted and the noise of the village which made sleep impossible.

It was not only the barking dogs which kept them awake, but strange Oriental music which was unpleasant to the European ear, although the Marquis had grown used to it.

The discomfort did not worry him very much, and the mystery of the East had an appeal which he knew of old was mesmeric.

It was the atmosphere of jasmine and sandalwood and the native people which made him feel in a way that he had "come home."

It was very different from what he felt in the grandeur of Quin or the luxury of his house in Park Lane.

As soon as Sabra had retired to bed, Kirkpatrick had said:

"Are you interested in sampling the exotic enjoyment which are doubtless available?"

The Marquis shook his head.

He knew exactly what Kirkpatrick meant, and for the moment had no desire to watch what would obviously be a show performed specially for strangers to Tunisia.

He had seen the genuine Ouled Naid dances which had a religious meaning behind them.

But this had in many places degenerated into a tawdry show with, as often as not, prostitutes from the Canebière replacing the native artists.

If he were to see anything of that sort, he wanted to be sure it was done for the Arabs themselves and not for strangers.

He looked with distaste at the rough wooden floor and the native bed which needed repairing and on which his own bedding had been placed.

He thought, too late, perhaps he had made a mistake in embarking on this expedition.

If he wanted to travel he could now afford to sail up the Nile in his own yacht or through the Suez Canal and down the Red Sea.

He was even more inclined than he had been previously to believe that Kirkpatrick's story of the treasure of El Djem was absolute nonsense.

He had learnt that Roman coins were frequently picked up all over Tunisia.

He had also read in the books he had brought that treasures which had been hidden in holes or passages continually came to light.

"I suppose I have been 'had for a mug!'" he told himself.

Then he knew that even if he was, he was enjoying the companionship of Kirkpatrick and was intrigued by the mysterious way in which his daughter behaved.

As he had no wish to linger longer than was absolutely necessary in the village, they left early the next morning and set off on which was to be a long day's journey.

It ended in an isolated plain where, if the maps were to be believed, there was no village.

The horses after a night's rest were sprightly, and the camels plodding behind them made light of the rough ground.

When they stopped for luncheon at what might have been described as an oasis, one of the camel-men approached them humbly and informed them that he was a fortune-teller.

Fortunately for the Marquis, for he was speaking Arabic in a strange manner, Sabra translated what he said, not to him, but to her father.

"Tell him we are not interested," Kirkpatrick answered. "I know my own fortune only too well."

"He says he has a distinct message for us."

It was obvious she was speaking insistently and the Marquis knew she wanted to hear what the man had to say.

"At least we can listen to him," he said good-humouredly, "and believe what we want to believe and ignore the rest."

"That is certainly a philosophical way of looking at things," Kirkpatrick remarked.

Sabra took what they had said as an answer in the affirmative and told the man that they would hear what he had to say.

He was a strange-looking creature, with a thin brown face, delicate nose and eye-brows, gleaming teeth, and eyes which had a strange beauty about them.

His turban was made of thick rope wound round and round a piece of white head-cloth.

It came out below the rope on each side of his face and served as a scarf for his long bare neck and chest.

The Marquis knew that rope turbans were worn only by people of the interior and he was a typical desert mystic.

The man squatted down, and, taking a handful of sand from a basket he carried with him he asked Sabra to hold it closely in her hands.

When she had done so, he spread it flat on the ground in front of him, made some passes over it, then carefully smoothed the surface of it again.

His movements were irritatingly slow.

The Marquis was just about to say that they should continue their journey, when he started marking in the sand queer geometrial designs which he traced with his long brown, white-nailed forefinger.

Finally he said, looking at Sabra:

"You have the eye of Allah and you look deep into the hearts of those you know. Allah is great. He is the Light of the World and some of His light shines through you."

He spoke in a strange, unworldly voice, and both Kirkpatrick and the Marquis were still as they listened.

"You will find happiness where you least expect it," he went on to Sabra, "but what you seek is not yours, it is Allah's and He holds what is His."

He paused, and the Marquis thought he had finished. Then he went on:

"Beware! When the moon sinks there is danger! Then only Allah can save you."

He rubbed out the markings in the sand, rose to his feet, and, very strangely, seemed about to leave without asking for any remuneration for his services.

The Marquis, taking three *sous* from his pocket, flung them on the ground, but the man hesitated as if he had no wish to touch the money.

Then a skinny brown arm came out of his white rag of a garment and he picked them up as disdainfully as if any remuneration were beneath him.

As he walked away, Kirkpatrick made a sound of disgust.

"That man gave me the creeps!" he said. "I do not believe a word of all that nonsense!"

"What did you think, Sabra?" the Marquis asked. "Was he genuine or was he just playing the usual Eastern game of extorting money from the tourists?"

She rose slowly from the ground, where the Marquis realised she had been sitting cross-legged, Eastern fashion.

"I think he . . . spoke the . . . truth," she said in a low voice as if the words were drawn from her.

"So you believe you have the eye of Allah?" the Marquis asked mockingly.

"We all have that if we wish to use it, but some people are deliberately blind."

Sabra's words were like an accusation, and without waiting for a reply, she walked to where her horse was waiting for her, held by an Arab.

"She is certainly unpredictable," the Marquis thought, as he had before.

Because it piqued him that any woman could be so indifferent, he was determined, somehow, before they reached the end of their journey, to make her aware of him.

Also, to make certain that she liked him for himself and perhaps trusted him.

They rode on, but before they had covered the number of miles the Marquis had planned, they stopped to rest for the night.

Their tents, which had been very expensive, were quickly and skillfully erected beside some straggling olive trees.

There was a rug laid down on the floor, and their sleeping-bags, which, because they also had cost a great deal of money, were extremely comfortable, were laid out for them.

Because there was no wind and it was very warm, dinner was eaten outside on a collapsible table which was carried by one of the camels.

There were chairs for them to sit on, and the food was delicious.

The Marquis had ordered from the hotel certain dishes on the advice of the head chef, which had travelled well, and the young kebab was tender and delicious.

He had already learnt that the Tunisian wines

were among the best produced in an Arab country.

Kirkpatrick had told him that one Monastery produced more than three million bottles of wine a year, red, white, and rosé.

It certainly seemed a very appropriate drink for where they were, and the Marquis even appreciated the fiery liqueur which was distilled from figs.

There was also plenty of fresh fruit which they had brought with them, and the fruit in Tunisia was not only delicious but also colourful.

The Marquis had taken a great deal of trouble to see that the cook who went with them was the very best obtainable in Tunis, and he had to admit he did miracles on the open fire.

They ate quite a number of different dishes before even Kirkpatrick said he had had enough.

In fact, he seemed replete with what he had eaten and imbibed and inclined to be sleepy.

The Marquis followed Sabra as she walked away from the lights which, now that darkness had fallen, illuminated their tents.

The animals were lying down a little way from them and the bearers were grouped round a fire.

It was not entirely dark, for the stars had come out like diamonds in the sky and there was a new moon which gave much more light than would have been expected in other parts of the world.

Away from the fire, Sabra seemed once again to be ethereal and not really human.

Walking beside her, the Marquis said:

"You have not yet told me if you are enjoying yourself, but I have a feeling that you are!"

"It is certainly very much more comfortable travelling with you than when Papa and I are alone."

"You are evading my question," the Marquis said. "I want to know if you are happy."

"Shall I say content for the moment."

He would have liked to see the expression on her face as she spoke in her soft, gentle, musical voice, which was different, he thought, from most other women's.

"Why are you 'splitting hairs'?" he enquired. "Why can you not say 'I am very happy and very grateful to my host'?"

"How do you know that would be . . . true?" she asked.

"What more do you want?" he enquired.

"Things which if I . . . explained them . . . you would not . . . understand."

"That is an infuriating reply," he said, "as you must know. Tell me. I think you will find I can understand most things."

"I decided a long time ago," Sabra said slowly, "it is quite impossible to have what one wants, and it is a great mistake to keep thinking about it and even worse to talk about it."

"That is a defeatist attitude," the Marquis retorted. "Tell me what you want and perhaps— who knows?—like a Genie in the Fairy-Stories, I can magic it to you!"

Sabra gave a little laugh.

"That is impossible!"

"The fortune-teller said you would find happiness."

She shrugged her shoulders.

"What he called 'happiness' maybe quite different from my idea of what it should be... and yours."

"Then tell me what you want."

"I have just said that that would be a mistake. For the moment I am content with the beauty of the night and the fact that Papa is no longer worried as to where the next meal is coming from."

"When the journey comes to an end," the Marquis said quietly, "what then?"

"You heard what the fortune-teller said. I must just pray to Allah and hope that He will look after me."

There was a little pause before the Marquis asked abruptly:

"Are you really so poor?"

"We are penniless."

"But why?"

"Why should you be interested?" she parried.

"Of course I am interested."

"We are only passing through your life transitorily, as you are well aware. It would be a great mistake for you to involve yourself more deeply with what we are and what we do.'"

"I would prefer to decide these matters for myself."

"I am sure that is what you will do, so there is

no point in my talking of what...might have been."

"I am asking you to tell me about yourself."

"You would find it very dull, and it is always a mistake to carry other people's troubles like a burden on your back."

The Marquis laughed.

"You are the most infuriating woman I have ever known! I ask you a direct question and you always come up with an evasive answer."

He paused before he continued:

"Of course I want to know about you—who you are, where you have come from, why you are living the life you are."

"And when you know all about me, and I assure you it is not very interesting, you will solve the riddle, put the last piece in the jig-saw, and then you will start looking around for another mystery."

"I have never heard such a ridiculous statement!"

"Is it so ridiculous? If you think you can read my thoughts, then I can read yours. You are interested simply because you dislike not knowing the truth, but truth inevitably, once you learn it, is disappointing."

"Is that your experience?"

"I suppose...so."

There was a dull note in her voice now that he did not understand.

Then he heard Kirkpatrick shout:

"Sabra, where are you? It is time you were in bed!"

"We must go back," the Marquis said, "but sooner or later, however much you try to prevent me, I intend to find an answer to all my questions."

As Sabra turned away from him, he heard her give a little chuckle.

"I hope when your curiosity is unsatisfied it does not keep you awake! *Bonsoir, Monsieur le Marquis!*"

With that she left him, running back silently over the sandy ground to where her father was waiting.

chapter four

THE Marquis thought he would never forget his first glimpse of Kairouan.

They approached it across a flat stony plain, dusty in dry weather, the camel-men told him, and one of the dreariest landscapes in the world.

The Marquis was just beginning to think it had been a mistake to come this way, when suddenly the horizon gleamed like a mirage.

It seemed to spring into existence under the very stones of the desert.

He did not speak, but riding on one side of him he heard Sabra exclaim beneath her breath:

"It looks like a... vision from *The Arabian Nights!*"

They rode on until they could see more clearly the minarets and the domes which the Marquis had read had all been built "as a witness and rampart of the faith of Mohammed."

Before they reached the city they came to a camel-market.

Although the Marquis had often seen one before, he was amused at the enthusiasm with which Sabra dismounted and hurried towards the herds of camels, both young and old.

Their coats were exactly the sandy colour of camel-hair overcoats.

Again the Marquis thought no animal could be more appropriate in the desert, with the innumerable uses to which it could be put.

They entered Kairouan through one of the main gates, *Bab-el Koukha*—the Gate of Peaches.

Moving slowly and with difficulty down the narrow, over-crowded streets, they passed the strange looking Mosque of the *Sabres*.

It had been founded by a holy man in the nineteenth century who got the Bey to pay for the six strange melon-shaped domes which decorated the top of the Mosque.

This information, of course, came from Kirkpatrick.

Although he related it amusingly, adding a little witticism of his own, the Marquis was aware that he had been told it first by his daughter.

It was difficult enough to reach the less crowded part of the town, but what was far more difficult was to find somewhere to stay.

The one hotel built after the French Occupation was full, and, in any case, looked so run-down and unpleasant that the Marquis refused to entertain even the idea of staying there.

Finally outside the walls they found a small resting-house that seemed clean and more or less quiet.

Without much enthusiasm, and because there appeared to be no alternative, the Marquis agreed they should stay there the night.

It was then they learned from the Proprietor of the resting-house that the town was so crowded because it was a special time for pilgrims to visit Kairouan.

Tomorrow was a Holy Day, when it was expected there would be in front of the great Mosque, something like 200,000 pilgrims.

The Marquis, however, was concerned at the moment with providing rest and refreshment for his caravan, including the camels and horses, and in getting food for themselves.

As usual in Tunisia it was easy to buy fresh vegetables and fruit from the market-place.

He sent one of the men hurrying to purchase some while he discussed with the cook what other food was available

With his eyes twinkling slightly, Kirkpatrick deliberately took no part in this.

He found a comfortable chair and settled himself in it with a bottle of golden wine at his side.

It did not surprise the Marquis when he thought about her to find that Sabra had disappeared.

He realised from the way she had stared at the

town that she was fascinated by the golden walls, and the minarets and domes of the same colour against the backdrop of a bright blue sky.

Because she seemed so self-sufficient, he did not worry about her going into the crowded streets as he would have done over any other young English girl.

"Anyway," he told himself, "if there is any worrying to be done over Sabra, it should be by her father, not me."

Only when they had finished what was at least an edible meal and he was aware that very shortly it would be dark did he say to Kirkpatrick:

"What has happened to your daughter?"

Kirkpatrick shrugged his shoulders

"She will turn up when she is hungry. She can, I assure you, look after herself."

The Marquis told himself that it would be a mistake to sound apprehensive.

He could not help feeling, however, that he would be perturbed about any Englishwoman who went off alone in an Arab City.

Kairouan might be, after Mecca and Jerusalem, the most Holy place for Moslem believers, but he was certain that its inhabitants were just as avaricious and unreliable as they would be in any other part of the country.

Finally, when Kirkpatrick went on drinking complacently, he rose to his feet and moved out of an open door onto the verandah.

From there he saw before him some scruffy, uncultivated land, and without even thinking where he was going, he walked down the steps and onto it.

He was aware that darkness was falling more quickly now that they were farther South

In a few minutes the daylight would have gone completely and the stars would be coming out.

Lights were already appearing in the houses and he could hear the noise of the streets and the clatter which always seemed to be part of the Arab way of life.

He walked on, aware that underneath his feet it was sandy, like the plain over which they had been passing all day, and the shrubs needed water.

Then he suddenly realised that somewhere near him a young voice was singing a tune he recognised.

He could hardly believe he was not imagining it, and he pushed his way through some Jasmine bushes and saw as he did so that he was now on another side of the resting-house.

In the light of a lantern which was hanging on a post he could see a number of children seated on the ground.

They were strangely quiet as they listened to the song which was being sung to them.

The Arab children were very beautiful with their coffee-coloured skins, oval faces, huge dark eyes, and long lashes that turned up in a fascinating way.

They were small, they were graceful, and until they grew older, they would look at the world wide-eyed, as if it were a wonderful place in which they would never be unhappy.

The Marquis had seen such children so often, and although he told himself he was absurdly sentimental, their beauty inevitably tugged at his heart.

Now, as he stood still to appreciate the children, some of them in rags and tatters, he saw seated under the lantern was Sabra, and it was she who was singing.

There was an Arab baby in her arms, and it took the Marquis a few moments to realise that the tune was one he had known ever since his own childhood and was a hymn.

Sabra was singing "All Things Bright and Beautiful" in Arabic.

He thought as he listened how skillfully she had translated the words and how convincingly they seemed to fit the music.

> *All things bright and beautiful,*
> *All creatures great and small,*
> *All things wise and wonderful*
> *And Allah made them all.*

She paused, and as the children clamoured for more, she made them sing it with her.

The tune was strange to them and therefore difficult, but the words were easy as she prompted them.

They sang in their high-pitched, shrill little

voices, and she joined in, leading and encouraging them.

Suddenly the Marquis realised with astonishment that she was not wearing her spectacles!

Now her eyes were revealed for the first time and he saw they were as large in her small face as the Arab children's and just as beautiful.

They were not dark, however, neither were they blue, but he was almost sure, although he could not see at all clearly, that they would be green with touches of gold.

The colour which reminded him of a clear stream in summer.

The song came to an end, and as the children again clamoured, as children would do in any country, for more, Sabra reluctantly rose to her feet.

She gave the baby she had been holding into the arms of an Arab girl who seemed a little older than the other children.

Then, as small hands went out to touch her and hold on to her dress, they moved with her towards the door of the resting-house.

The Marquis could hear her soft musical voice as she told them she would try to come back and sing for them again.

But she said:

"I am a traveler, and you understand that travellers cannot stay long."

She put her hands on the heads of one or two of the children running round her, then she said the word every Arab man uses when he says "good-bye" to a friend.

"*Marhaba*—Allah go with you."

As she reached the doorway, the children shouted almost in unison:

"*Marhaba—Marhaba,*" before she vanished.

It had been a strange scene, totally unexpected but the Marquis thought enchanting.

As he walked back the way he had come, he thought perceptively that he now understood why Sabra wore tinted spectacles.

If she did not wear them it would be impossible for any man to ignore her, and he was sure she had discovered this for herself and had used them as a weapon of defence.

He walked up the steps onto the verandah, then into the room which he had persuaded the resting-house keeper to allot them as a private Sitting-Room.

Sabra was already sitting at the table.

The servants were bringing her dishes fresh from the kitchen.

There was also on the table some food which the Marquis had ordered to be purchased from the best shops in the City.

As he entered through the glass door which also served as a window, he was aware that she was wearing her glasses.

She had also, he knew, withdrawn once again into herself.

He wondered if he should tell her what he had seen.

Then he decided it might embarrass her and merely sat down in an armchair opposite Kirkpatrick, who started a conversation about the distance they would have to travel the next day.

"We have already covered ninety-seven miles since we left Tunis," he said, "and we have, in fact, far fewer to go to reach El Djem."

"I only hope the going will be good," the Marquis replied.

While he spoke, he was, in fact, watching Sabra.

He thought there was a smile on her lips he had not seen before and knew it was because she had been with the children and it had made her happy.

'What an extraordinary girl she is!' he thought to himself. 'Why will she not talk to me without being mysterious?'

Because he could not help being curious, he rose to his feet to fetch another bottle of wine.

Holding it in his hand, he sat down at the table where Sabra was eating.

"What do you want to do?" he asked. "Stay here tomorrow, or push on towards El Djem?"

"I think that is for you to decide," Sabra answered. "It is your expedition, not mine!"

"But you must have some feelings in the matter?" the Marquis persisted.

"They are hardly . . . important."

"That is for me to say. I have asked you a question and I would like an answer."

"Very well, then," Sabra said. "I think, because

it would be a mistake for our expedition to take too long, that we should, as you put it, 'push on.'"

The Marquis raised his eye-brows.

"Why should our Expedition not take a long time?"

"You know the ... answer to ... that!"

"Can you really be reminding me of my duty?" the Marquis enquired.

She did not answer but peeled a pomegranate delicately, her eyes on its rose-tinted skin.

"I asked you a question," he said, thinking it was something he was continually saying since he had met her.

She smiled and he knew that her large, expressive eyes were smiling as she said:

"It is very English always to accentuate the obvious. If you can read my thoughts, I can read yours, and you know what I mean without my putting it into words."

"If you talk to me like that," the Marquis remarked, "I shall stay here for a week—perhaps two!"

Sabra laughed, and it was a very attractive sound.

"That would not punish me," she replied.

He knew she was thinking of the children, and that she would like to sing to them again.

Then before he could go on talking to her as he wanted to do, she rose to her feet saying:

"I am tired, Papa, so I am going to bed."

"Very sensible, my dear," Kirkpatrick agreed,

"and it is what I have every intention of doing myself!"

As Sabra walked towards the door, the Marquis was watching her, but he did not move.

She looked at him, then almost mockingly she said:

"Goodnight, My Lord. *Mektoub*."

The Marquis knew that the word *mektoub* translated meant "it is written" and was the word of the Prophet.

It was also used to cover a lot of inefficiency and laziness in the Arab world, which was very far from the Prophet's intentions.

It more often than not meant a human lack of will and effort rather than a resigned submission to a Sublime Will.

He knew exactly what Sabra meant by saying it to him, and he was amused by her impertinence.

At the same time he had to admit wryly to himself that she was making it very clear that if he behaved as he ought to, he would return to England as quickly as possible.

'Damn the girl!' he thought. 'I will not be pressured into doing something I have no wish to do!'

Nevertheless, he found himself giving orders that they would leave Kairouan the next day and press on towards El Djem.

It was not, however, as easy as it sounded.

The going was rough, and after three nights in their tents, they hoped after an early start on the next day to reach El Djem before nightfall.

They had not ridden far, when the Marquis noticed in the distance what he thought was a sand-storm approaching them.

There was a huge greyish cloud rising about twenty feet above the ground and sweeping towards them in a great arc which stretched both to the right and to the left as far as the eye could see.

He was just going to ask the leader of the caravan what he thought they should do, knowing that a sand-storm could be very unpleasant, when Sabra gave a cry of "Locusts!"

For a moment he turned his head to stare at her.

Then, as she jumped down from her horse and turned it round with its back towards the cloud, he realised that the camels were being treated in the same way, and knew that there was no time to be lost.

He dismounted quickly and turned his horse as Sabra had done hers, and saw that Kirkpatrick was following his example.

They then crouched down on the ground with their heads as low as possible, and a second later the locusts were over them.

He knew from previous encounters with locusts that if they hit a man in the face, they could easily give him a black eye.

Fortunately, however, the locusts were on the move and they flew over them, making a strange sound as they went.

Then almost as quickly as they had come they disappeared into the distance, leaving only a few of their number on the horses' and camels' backs and on their own shoulders and heads.

"We always seem to run into locusts around here," the head camel-driver said cheerily. "It is the Will of Allah and there is nothing we can do about it."

"Nothing at all," the Marquis agreed.

He watched while Kirkpatrick brushed down his daugher's back, she being more concerned with her horse than with herself.

They rode on and, as the Marquis had hoped, had their first glimpse of El Djem in the afternoon.

It appeared on the horizon of the featureless plain like a gigantic ship on an empty ocean.

He was aware that all the later Roman Amphitheatres had been designed after the pattern of the great Coliseum in Rome, although they did not agree in the details and construction.

The sun and time had baked the limestone of which the Amphitheatre was built to a lovely honey colour.

It was, he thought, as exciting and surprising as seeing the Great Pyramids of Egypt for the first time.

"It is so... big!" Sabra murmured as if she spoke to herself rather than to him.

It was certainly a tremendous size and more impressive because from a distance it appeared to be completely isolated.

As they drew nearer they could see how lofty it was.

The Marquis had read in one of the guide books that the Amphitheatre rose to a height of 120 feet and it could hold seventy-thousand spectators.

Behind it they discovered a few roughly constructed Arab houses, most of them built with stones from the Amphitheatre itself.

The Marquis found it infuriating to learn that until the seventeenth century it was complete and undamaged. Then an Arab moved into the arcades under the rising rows of seats.

A bandit gang took refuge amongst them, barricading the gates against the Bey's men, who were after them, so that they had to pull down some of the outer wall to get them out.

Once this had happened, the local people helped themselves to the available stones to build houses, so now there were gaps in the wall and much of the galleries had gone.

But the Marquis was not prepared to criticise when Sabra was saying breathlessly:

"It is . . . wonderful! It is just what I thought it would be like but . . . it is even more . . . exciting!"

"I suggest," Kirkpatrick said in a practical tone, "before we go into eulogies over what we have come to find, that we discover where it would be best to pitch our tents and make ourselves comfortable for the night."

The Marquis knew this meant that Kirkpatrick was longing for a drink.

He could, however, be comforted by the thought that one of the camels carried a great number of bottles of wine as well as the food they had brought with them.

He gave the order and the camel-drivers hurried to unload their beasts and erect the tents on a clear piece of ground, shielded by a few scraggy olive trees.

As they were doing so, Kirkpatrick found himself a comfortable place to sit and a bottle of wine with which to alleviate the hardships of the journey.

The Marquis was aware that Sabra was looking longingly at the Amphitheatre.

"Shall we go to look at it before it grows too dark?" he suggested, and was rewarded with one of her rare but brilliant smiles.

He knew as they walked together to the entrance that she was really excited.

He thought that few women he had known in the past would have been so thrilled at what to them would have been just a forgotten ruin.

The moment they entered the Amphitheatre and started to walk along the galleries where once the Roman Settlers sat to watch human beings struggling against frenzied wild beasts, Sabra stepped back into the past.

It was nothing that she said, but the Marquis felt she had gone away from him into a world that was as real to her as the one in which she was actually living.

Reading her thoughts, he was aware that she was seeing the seats filled with the shouting, excited, screaming spectators.

Then, as they stopped in the centre of the Amphitheatre and looked down into the arena, he was aware that Sabra was trembling.

He knew that she was visualising men and women fighting against and fleeing from the lions, tigers, and bears that were destroying them.

There was the smell of warm blood and it was intoxicating into a frenzy the vast crowd of spectators.

He was not sure how she knew all this, and yet for the moment he could see it all through Sabra's eyes and was aware of how it distressed and frightened her.

She could not escape from it, but was forced, even as the Roman women had been forced, to watch the horror that was taking place for their delectation.

She had come without a hat, and now in the last glow of the evening her hair seemed against the bare stone to shine as if it held the light of the sun.

It flashed through the Marquis's mind that she might almost be the reincarnation of the famous Queen Kahena, who had led a victorious army.

Thanks to her diplomacy, several Berber tribes had forgotten their mutual rivalry and followed her.

She had then led them in revolt to Carthage and won a battle. El Djem became her headquarters and was turned into a fortress.

Queen Kahena was renowned for her beauty, and became more and more powerful through a series of successful campaigns, always returning to El Djem in triumph.

The Marquis remembered reading how in A.D. 703 the Muslims under a General Hassan swore to bring the Queen to her knees.

Her fortune changed and she suffered defeat after defeat, but still she retained El Djem.

When her forces could no longer hold out, they begged her to go into hiding, but she would not agree to do this.

When all was lost, rather than be captured she plunged her own sword into her breast.

The General, not appeased by this gesture, cut off her head.

He sent it in a basket studded with jewels as a token of fidelity to the Caliph of Baghdad.

The story flashed through the Marquis's mind.

He thought that if Sabra were in the same position, like the Queen she would fight valiantly and would never surrender.

Then as he stood looking at her, suddenly she pulled off her disfiguring spectacles and he saw that tears were running down her cheeks.

Instinctively, without thinking, he put his arms around her and she turned her face against his shoulder.

"It is . . . horrible! Bestial!" she murmured in a voice he could hardly hear, but there was no mistaking its tone of horror.

"Those poor . . . people! How can they . . . fight animals?"

She was trembling and he knew that she was

feeling as if she herself were in the arena being torn to pieces.

"It is all over," he said gently, "and it happened a long time ago. Instead, I was thinking that you might have been Queen Kahena in a previous life."

Sabra was listening, and she did not tremble quite so violently as she said with a catch in her throat:

"She...stood her...ground and did not... surrender."

"She did not surrender," the Marquis replied softly, "and she was very brave."

"I will...think about her...and not about... the victims who were torn to...pieces and... eaten."

The words came jerkily from between Sabra's lips.

"Think of yourself as Queen Kahena," he said. "I am sure, since she was beautiful, that you are very like her."

The way he spoke was so surprising that Sabra raised her head from his shoulder to look up at him.

He thought in the last dying light that no one could be more lovely.

Her long eyelashes were wet from her tears, which also stained her cheeks. Her eyes were the colour he had thought they would be, green flecked with gold.

Then, as her lips trembled with the emotions that had shaken her, the Marquis forgot everything except that she was a woman and he was holding her in his arms.

Without thinking his lips came down on hers.

He knew as he kissed her and held her captive that it seemed in the strangeness of the haunted Amphitheatre as if it had been ordained since the beginning of time.

Sabra had the same feeling, and it was so much part of her imagination, so much part of what she had just felt that she was not certain whether she was one of the screaming victims being devoured by the lions and tigers, as the Marquis had suggested, or Queen Kahena herself.

All she knew was that he overwhelmed her and his lips awoke in her strange feelings she had never known.

At the same time, in a way they were part of her dreams and what she had always sensed she would find.

Then, as his arms tightened and his lips having at first been gentle became more demanding, she felt as if he drew her heart and soul from her body and made them his.

She could feel a light moving like a living stream through her body into her breast and up from her throat to her lips.

The light was part of the Marquis.

There were flames of fire within it, and it was so perfect, so Divine, that she knew it was what she had always sought.

The Marquis raised his head to look at her, feeling he must have known he would see an incredible radiance in her eyes.

She was transfigured, seeming no longer human but Divine.

Then he was kissing her again: kissing her fiercely, demandingly, as if he wanted to conquer her and make her completely and absolutely his prisoner.

Sabra was not afraid. She knew only that the emotions he evoked in her were so perfect, so sublime that it was what she had sought in her prayers.

It was as if he took the stars from the sky and put them in her breast, then lifted her up amongst them.

His kisses gave her an ecstatic rapture and at the same time, in their intensity, almost a physical pain so that she quivered against him, and the Marquis knew that now it was not with fear.

He kissed her until darkness fell, and because he realised the danger they might be in on the gallery with yawning, cave-like alcoves and a holed floor he took Sabra's hand in his.

Because it would be easy to fall and break a leg, he led her slowly back the way they had come.

Only then did Sabra stop to look back, and as she did so she knew that their relationship had changed.

The Marquis was not certain, now that he was back to reality, whether what had occurred was wise or unwise.

Then, as he drew Sabra away from the Amphitheatre onto the rough road, there was light from the native houses which would guide them back to where they were camped.

He was aware that he carried, almost without thinking, Sabra's spectacles.

She had taken them from her eyes and he thought that perhaps the fact she had done so was symbolic.

Then he was afraid to admit to himself what it signified.

chapter five

In the darkness of his tent, the Marquis lay thinking that kissing Sabra had been an unusually exciting experience, but perhaps it had been a mistake.

He had no wish to become involved with a woman while he was on an expedition of this sort.

It had never occurred to him until they were in the Amphitheatre that Sabra was, in fact, extremely attractive.

As she had trembled against him, he was bemused and bewildered by the strange emotions he was experiencing.

Then he had found it impossible not to be aware of the softness of her body against his, and that she was crying against his shoulder.

Impulsively, he had reached out to comfort her

and felt himself deeply moved by the feeling the Amphitheatre had evoked in her.

Because he could read her thoughts, he had felt almost as she did the overwhelming intimations of the past.

He could not explain it to himself, but he had felt like Sabra that he could hear the shouting, the screaming, the intense excitement of those who watched.

He could almost see, as Sabra was doing, the human beings struggling against the lions and tigers, and trying to elude the bears.

Their blood caused by the animals' claws to pour down their naked bodies.

He could understand how much it horrified her.

Yet some part of his mind also understood the frenzied excitement of the crowd intoxicated by the smell of blood.

Then, as he thought of it, he asked himself how it was possible that anyone as young as Sabra could have the gift of clairvoyance, if that was the name for it.

It had carried her back to the past, and influenced him as well, so that he could hear with her ears and see with her eyes.

He wanted to tell himself it was all an illusion, that he had been merely carried away by the magnificence of the Amphitheatre.

What was more, being tired from the journey had made him easily susceptible to such nonsense.

But he knew that was untrue, and as he

thought back, he remembered that it was without meaning to that he had kissed Sabra.

He had known that she responded to his lips with her whole body, and, he suspected, her heart.

His cynical mind, which had been induced in him from a very early age by his father, told him that what had happened was just something entirely physical and the sooner he forgot it the better.

But it was untrue, and it was important to believe, as his father would have sneeringly asserted, that Sabra had deliberately incited him.

Like all women, he would have said, she had wanted to attract and capture a man, especially one as important as himself.

The Marquis knew, if he was honest, that Sabra, on the contrary, avoided him as much as possible on their journey.

When she had turned to him with the tears streaming down her face and trembling at what she could see and hear in the ruins of the Amphitheatre, she had not been thinking of him as a man.

She had turned to him merely as some protection from her own emotions, which was not normal nor in any way contrived by a desire to involve him.

Then, when she turned her face up to him, she had looked so irresistibly attractive and at the same time pathetic with the tears in her eyes and on her cheeks, he had acted, the Marquis told himself, as any man would have done in the same position.

However, it was a mistake, a great mistake, and he was not certain for the moment how he could rectify it.

There was no need to do anything when they returned to the camp, for Sabra had slipped silently away from him into her tent.

When the Marquis looked in on her father, he had seen that Kirkpatrick, seated in a chair with a half-empty bottle of wine beside him, was asleep.

The Marquis had therefore gone to his own tent, and only when supper was ready had he sent one of the servants to tell Kirkpatrick and Sabra that he was waiting for them.

He was not surprised, but knew it was what he might have expected, when Sabra did not appear.

"I expect she is tired," Kirkpatrick said complacently, and the Marquis, having no intention of confiding in him, agreed.

He had gone to bed early because he wanted to think about what had happened and ask himself how such a thing was possible.

He had always imagined when his friends had described to him similar experiences that they must be slightly deranged.

Alternatively, they had drunk too much in a climate where strong liquor was a mistake.

Of course there was always the suspicion that they were exaggerating or simply lying to make themselves appear more important.

There were also people who swore they had

seen ghosts, who believed in the predictions of astrologers.

Charletans who preyed on those who were susceptible to such influences in a manner that the Marquis thought extremely reprehensible.

But where Sabra was concerned, he felt that to her it was all true and, although he hated to admit it, it had happened to him also, albeit in a lesser and not so violent way.

He did not repudiate it, but he wanted to find a logical explanation of why it had happened.

When he thought about it, he knew it was impossible to "talk away" something which quite certainly he would never forget.

He would also find it difficult to forget the softness, the innocence, and the purity of Sabra's lips.

He had known when he saw her singing to the children outside the resting-house that he was no longer arguing and contending with an unpredictable, rather irritating young woman who amused him because she deliberately pretended to be mysterious.

Then the Marquis paused.

It was difficult to find words, or rather he found he had no wish to describe to himself what he felt about Sabra now.

He tossed and turned and found it very difficult to sleep; in fact, sleep came only just before dawn.

Although he was not aware of it, Sabra had risen early to watch the sun coming up over the plain.

She had seen on the journey South that the

plains were even more beautiful and more breath-taking than the mountains which they had passed soon after leaving Tunis.

Now the scenery was so beautiful that she felt as if it invaded her whole body and she became a part of it.

There were innumerable meadow flowers which bloomed in tropical abundance between the bright green clumps of grass and covered them with a rosy-orange colour, or with patches of white.

The whole ground in front of her looked like a gigantic Oriental carpet.

She thought it was very likely that the Persians and Syrians had taken ideas for their famous car-pets from the magnificence of the patterns offered to them here by Nature.

As they wove passages from the Koran into the patterns of their many-coloured textures, so this natural carpet seemed to Sabra to embody the writings of the ancient Prophets.

It was so lovely under the gold of the rising sun that she felt herself transported into a world she had never known but always sensed was there, if only she could find it.

As her whole body throbbed with a strange emotion, it was inevitably mixed in her mind with the sensations the Marquis had aroused in her the previous evening.

Sabra had never been kissed before.

She had always eluded and treated with disdain

the numerous men who, from the moment she had grown up, had attempted to fondle her.

It was because she shrank from the look in their eyes and from their hands reaching out to touch her that she had bought herself the tinted spectacles and insisted upon wearing them.

Her father was furious because without really putting it into words even to himself, he found it useful that men should be attracted to his daughter.

It made them blind to what he intended until it was too late to "pass by on the other side," as he might have put it.

Kirkpatrick had raged at Sabra, telling her that if she would not do as he told her, he would put her in an Orphanage and forget about her.

But she had only laughed at him, and he knew she had a strength and an obstinacy which he would be unable to break.

After many recriminations he merely sulkily accepted that she would behave as she wished to and nothing he could say would change her mind.

He had once hit her, and she had said:

"If you do that, Papa, I shall leave you. I promised Mama I would look after you and that is what I am trying to do."

She paused a moment before continuing:

"But I will not act as a lure, or bait, if you prefer the word, for the men from whom you wish to extract money, and I personally will accept nothing from them—nothing at all!"

"In which case you will go naked and starve!" Kirkpatrick had snapped.

Sabra had accepted food because it was impossible not to do so when her father was there and they ate in some grand restaurant but could not afford breakfast.

But she took care never to be alone with any man.

Determinedly, and to Kirkpatrick infuriatingly, she wore only clothes that she had bought with the money he gave her. She would not accept presents of any sort from the men with whom he became involved.

"You little fool!" he roared at her once when she had refused a bracelet she had been offered.

He would have sold it later and nobody knew better than Sabra did that they needed the money.

"How was I expected to pay for it?" Sabra had asked scathingly, and her father had not answered.

It had been a difficult life and to Sabra a miserable one without her mother.

Yet there were moments like now when everything was worthwhile and she would not have missed it for all the security and comfort she longed for at other times.

The beauty of the plain was, she thought, engraved on her very soul.

When the expedition was over and once again her father was looking for a rich man to pay for them both, she would remember the meadow flowers.

They were like a living carpet under a sunlit sky, and nothing else would seem to matter.

Then a voice in her mind asked the question:

"And what else will you remember?"

If the Marquis had lain awake last night in the darkness of his tent, so had Sabra.

It was impossible for her not to continue to quiver with the ecstasy he had aroused in her and which had been like a burning light sweeping through her body at the touch of his lips.

It was part of the beauty of all the loveliness she had seen recently, like the bougainvillaea and the hybiscus in the garden of the Villa.

There was the blue of the Mediterranean and their first glimpse of the orange-coloured walls of Kairouan.

There were pictures which she knew she would see and go on seeing and which no one could take away from her and they were hers for eternity.

Only as the sun began to grow hot did she realise she must go back.

As she turned round she saw again the Amphitheatre still proudly proclaiming the power of Rome, even though almost two thousand years had elapsed.

Then she remembered how the Marquis had said she might have been Queen Kahena.

She wondered if given the same circumstances she would have had the strength to fight and go on fighting for what she believed was right as the Queen had done.

She knew then that in her own small way she had been fighting a difficult battle ever since her mother had died.

She had fought to save herself from being exploited by her father, and to save him from becoming even more of a rascal than he was already.

It was a task which most women would have found impossible, and often Sabra cried at night into her pillow, saying hopelessly:

"I have . . . failed you . . . Mama . . . I cannot do as . . . you wished."

But she had known in the morning that a strength was given to her to continue, to go on fighting and never give in.

Now, as she looked at the great Amphitheatre, she told herself that if it could survive for so many centuries, so could she.

When she walked back towards the camp she was holding her chin high.

The men had finished breakfast and she could see that her father and the Marquis were sitting a little way from the tent under some olive trees talking earnestly.

She guessed they were deciding exactly how they should set about the search for the treasure which her father was convinced was waiting for them.

Actually, she thought scornfully that it was like so many of his "pipe dreams."

She would be very surprised if however hard they dug they would find anything but a few coins.

Or perhaps the bones of one of the miserable creatures who had been torn to death in the Amphitheatre.

She knew, however, it would be a mistake to express her misgivings either to the Marquis or to her father.

She sat down at the breakfast-table and as she did so sent the Berber boy who was waiting on her to ask the Marquis for her spectacles.

She had not thought about them until she woke.

Then, when she had dressed, she had put out her hand for them, only to remember that the Marquis had carried them away when they left the Amphitheatre.

The boy did as he was told.

As she drank the coffee and ate a little of the bread which was already stale, as they had brought it with them and had not yet made any purchases in the village, the Marquis looked towards her.

He said something to the boy, who hurried back to her.

What he said in Arabic made Sabra frown. He told her that the Marquis had mislaid the spectacles and he thought anyway she did not need them.

"I *do* need them!" she wanted to argue, then knew that the Marquis was right.

She had used them as a disguise and as a weapon against men who she had no wish to touch her.

Yet she could not say that of the Marquis when the wonder of his kiss had remained with her all night.

She knew she would not forget it today or any day.

There was now no barrier between them, nor did she wish him to find her unattractive.

He was so different from any man she had known before that Sabra could hardly believe her own feelings.

She felt herself blush as she drank a little more coffee and ate some of the fruit which was fresh and delicious.

Then once again she walked away from the camp to look at the Amphitheatre from a different angle, and did not join the two men until she heard her father calling her.

Reluctantly, because she felt shy in stepping from her fanciful world back into reality, she moved through the meadow flowers to where they were sitting in the shade.

The Marquis, watching her approach them, thought she looked like a young goddess in an Elysian field.

Despite his resolution to behave as if nothing unusual had happened between them, he found himself staring at her.

He was thinking that her hair was the most perfect colour he had ever seen on any woman.

Sabra had eaten her breakfast without covering her head with her broad-brimmed hat.

Now she carried it in her hand, feeling the

warmth of the sun on her head and supremely unaware that she was doing anything unwise, until her father said sharply:

"For God's sake, child, put on your hat! I do not want you down with sunstroke!"

Sabra obeyed him, and the Marquis felt as if he were abruptly jerked back into normality.

"Good morning, Sabra!" he said in his usual somewhat dry tones. "Your father and I have been working out how we shall approach this treasure in which he is interested."

He paused before he continued:

"We think it would be a mistake to be seen digging in the daylight."

Sabra looked away from him before she answered:

"I am sure . . . you are . . . right. If you do . . . discover anything, the local inhabitants would certainly . . . expect . . . their share."

"That is exactly what I thought," Kirkpatrick intervened. "So what we have to do is to start our excavations just before it gets dark, when most people will be in their houses."

Her father stopped speaking and looked at her.

"The Marquis and I will reconnoitre the site alone, which is only a few hundred yards from here."

"And where is that?" Sabra enquired.

"As I have said, my informant told me it was near a ruined Temple," her father answered impatiently, "and as far as we can ascertain, except for the Amphitheatre, there is only one other ruin."

He looked at her sternly before he went on:

"It consists of what remain of a few Roman Pillars. The ground there is soft and should present no difficulties to able-bodied men."

"You do not intend to tell the camel-drivers what you mean to do?" Sabra asked.

"We have discussed that," Kirkpatrick replied, "and we think it would be a mistake, although later, should we find anything, we will tell Bachir."

He was the head of the caravan and a middle-aged man whom Sabra thought they could trust.

She herself, however, preferred Achmet, a younger man who had taken it upon himself to be the personal servant of both her father and the Marquis.

He went out of his way also to do everything possible for her.

He was a Berber with really fine features and large dark eloquent eyes.

He would bring her flowers or fruit as a small gift whenever they stopped in a town.

As they passed, he would pick her a wild orchid, or one or two strange but very beautiful flowers for which no one seemed to have a name.

She thought of suggesting that they might trust Achmet, then thought it would be a mistake for her to interfere.

She understood that her father and the Marquis were afraid that if one man knew of the treasure, there would be a dozen digging away.

Perhaps even stealing the spoils before they could have a chance of seeing what was there.

"So that is our plan," Kirkpatrick went on, "and I suggest that like the camels, we have a quiet and easy day and reserve our strength."

"I agree with you," the Marquis said.

He was, however, aware even before they had finished speaking that Sabra had moved away, and he knew she was going to the Amphitheatre.

He wondered if he should follow her, then decided it would be a mistake.

Last night they had been carried away by wild emotions, which now seemed in retrospect not only unaccountable, but even reprehensible.

He therefore went to his tent.

After instructing Achmet to put a chair for him in the shade, he took two of the books he had brought with him from the yacht and started to read about El Djem, with its long and fascinating history.

Although the book was well written, with many illustrations, he found it could not hold him.

Instead, he was thinking of Sabra and what she was feeling as she wandered round the galleries and remembered not only what had happened in the past but what she had seen and heard last night.

Sabra, as it happened, was not wandering, as the Marquis thought she was doing.

Instead, she was sitting on the second gallery,

which appeared to be the safest and least damaged.

She was trying to remember all she had read about El Djem without once again being involved in the agonies and death throes of those who had perished in the building.

What had happened last night now seemed like a dream, except that the Marquis had not vanished but was still there, very much alive.

Despite her determination to behave ordinarily, she felt her whole being reaching out towards him.

She knew that she wanted more than she had ever wanted anything before to be with him, to talk to him, and, if she were truthful, for him to kiss her again.

'I suppose this is love,' she thought.

It was something she had never expected to find with any man to whom her father had introduced her.

She despised them, hated them, and had deliberately, as the Marquis sensed, withdrawn into herself so that they could not encroach on her.

Now the very last man she might have expected to love, and one she had fought bitterly with her father to avoid, had captured her heart.

It was no longer hers but his.

"I love him!" she whispered.

But he must never be aware of her feelings because it would be something he would not wish to hear.

Sabra was wise enough to realise that a man

like the Marquis, with his great position in England, his distinguished title, and what she was sure was a long experience of women, would never wish to become involved with the daughter of a man like Kirkpatrick.

She had not missed through her tinted spectacles the little twist to his lips when her father was too obvious in his efforts to captivate the Marquis's interest and force himself upon him.

She had despised him, too, for giving in so easily and offering them not only the first decent meal they had had for a long time but also accommodation in his Villa.

"How can you be such a fool," she had wanted to ask the Marquis, "as not to realise that Papa is 'conning' you as he has 'conned' so many other men?"

Then, as they finished dinner, she was aware that the Marquis was not deceived by her father.

He had accepted his ridiculous story because he wanted to do so, and was also prepared not only to offer them his hospitality, but a great many other things as well.

When the men had come back from Nice, having bought what they both thought they would need on their expedition, Sabra found that her father had included a pair of white trousers to wear on the yacht.

Also what Officers of the Brigade of Guards called a "boating-jacket," with gold buttons and a peaked cap to wear with it.

"How can you impose on the Marquis by pretending that is necessary for our voyage to Tunisia!" she demanded scornfully. "We shall not be at sea for more than two days!"

"How do you know?" her father had replied airily. "We shall have to come back again and we might even be able to persuade our noble host to have a look at Constantinople."

"What are you suggesting he find there? A Sultan's jewel in a forgotten minaret?" Sabra asked scathingly.

Her father laughed.

"It is certainly an idea which I shall consider."

Sabra had not answered, but merely walked out of his bedroom and shut the door sharply behind her.

She had known as she went to her own comfortable room that her father was only laughing at her.

He would never understand that she found his behaviour degrading.

She felt herself wince at every penny some idiotic man spent on them just because her father manipulated him so cleverly.

"They have it and we want it," her father had said often enough, as if that explained everything satisfactorily.

She knew it was no use arguing with him or suggesting that any other way of life would be preferable to the one they were living.

Now, unexpectedly, when she had never dreamt that such a thing would happen, she had fallen in love with one of the men who had listened like an idiot to her father, as if to the beguiling music of the "Pied Piper."

She had sometimes hoped that one day she would be fortunate enough to find someone she loved and who would love her.

A man she could marry and live with, perhaps in a cottage in the quietness of the countryside.

He would give her a home, and that was what she wanted above everything else.

Sabra sat in the Amphitheatre until hunger drove her back to the camp.

Luncheon was an unexpectedly palatable meal.

The cook had found a man who had shot three quails earlier that morning and had bought them from him.

A woman had baked some quite edible bread, although it was the Eastern sort which had no relation to the English bread that Sabra dreamed of eating in her imaginary cottage.

There were also fresh vegetables which were delicious.

When Sabra first saw them, she had thought nothing could be more beautiful than their colours as they glowed in a tiny shop in the centre of Tunis.

There was some good wine to drink because her father had seen to that.

Although she said very little, she was vividly conscious of the Marquis looking exceedingly handsome.

She thought he looked more relaxed and less

cynical and sarcastic than he had been when they crossed the Mediterranean.

"Even if he finds nothing," she told herself, "it will have been well worthwhile from his point of view because he has been amused."

Then she realised that he was deliberately avoiding meeting her eyes.

Suddenly she felt as if the golden sunshine had vanished and instead she was clutched by an icy hand.

It was about half past three in the afternoon, when her father signalled it was time for them to move towards their objective.

The camels were lying down, as they had been ever since they had arrived.

Only their heads were moving as they watched what was happening around them, which at the moment was very little.

The horses were cropping the grass, and the men in charge of them were seated in the shade of the olive trees either sleeping or talking to each other in low voices.

The curiosity their party had aroused in the village when they first arrived seemed to have abated.

Now even the small boys no longer appeared to be curious about them.

It was more than likely, however, that they would reappear at dinner, when there might be a chance for them to snatch a few scraps of food and perhaps some unwanted fruit.

Casually, as if there were no reason to hurry,

Kirkpatrick and the Marquis walked away from the camp.

They were followed a little distance behind them by Sabra.

The ruined Temple they had discovered was on the other side of the Amphitheatre.

Unless someone was watching for them, they could not be seen by the people in the Arab houses or by their own servants.

They reached the ruined Temple, of which only two Ionic columns were standing, the rest being scattered on the ground.

Sabra suddenly realised that when they had walked away from their tents her father and the Marquis had each carried a spade close against their chests.

They were half-covered by their loose coats so that no one watching would have any idea the two men had any such implements with them.

As they put their spades down on the ground and took off their coats, Sabra was aware of how very strong and masculine the Marquis looked in his shirt-sleeves.

She quickly glanced away from him, embarrassed by her own thoughts, and sat down in the thick grass some distance away from where they were working.

As she did so she looked over the vast, empty plain.

She found herself thinking of how lonely and homesick the women who had accompanied the

Romans must have felt when they were so far away from home.

For the men there was always the thrill and excitement of conquering and exploring a new land and eventually making it prosperous.

For a woman there was only the difficulty of making a home, of educating her children, and trying to bring into a primitive atmosphere the principles and civilisation of Rome.

'They must have been very, very lonely,' Sabra thought.

She forgot her father and the Marquis as she found herself lost in the feelings of the exiles who would perhaps never see their parents or friends they had loved again.

She must have been day-dreaming, for nearly an hour had passed before she realised that the sun had lost its strength and there was a hint of darkness in the sky.

It would be dark in half-an-hour, she decided.

Then she knew that was when her father and the Marquis would give up working until another day, or else wait until the moon rose.

It would have made them too conspicuous to work by the light of lanterns or flares.

'I ought to go to tell them to hurry,' she thought, but then felt no wish to leave the comfort of the place where she was lying.

She realised, as if for the first time, that the grass was massed with small flowers and between the plants there was sand.

Then she saw sliding through the sand a small, very small green lizard.

She moved forward, stretching herself out so that she could watch its progress more closely, thinking how attractive its colour was and how quick its movements as it scurried between the plants.

It was entrancing to watch.

Then, as she lay there, the lizard suddenly vanished and she looked up to see approaching over the flat plain there were some horsemen.

There were six of them, obviously Bedouins, and she wondered where they had come from and where they were going.

She did not move as they galloped straight up to where her father and the Marquis were digging with, by this time, only the upper part of their bodies showing above the ground.

The leading Bedouin was characteristically tall, robust, a fine-looking man, and Sabra knew his face would be sun-tanned and his eyes fiery.

He was wearing a burnous with a hood which he had drawn low over his forehead and which he wore over his fez, with its long tassle, and wound over it a white turban.

She guessed, because she had read quite a lot about Bedouins, that he would be wearing riding-boots of red or yellow Morocco leather.

She had, however, little time in which to stare at him before, to her horror, she saw him bend down and pull her father out of the trench in which he was digging.

She heard her father shout.

As he did so, two other Bedouins without dismounting dragged the Marquis also from the trench.

He resisted violently, but caught unawares and outnumbered, he was inevitably over-powered.

One of them took the spade from his hand and threw it disdainfully onto the ground.

Then before Sabra could really take in what was happening, both men were enveloped in black burnouses, and ropes were wound round them with a swiftness that seemed almost incredible.

In what was not more than a few seconds they were thrown, trussed and helpless, over the saddles of two horses.

The Bedouins, following their leader, turned back the way they had come.

By the time Sabra had sat up to watch them go, they had vanished into the darkening distance.

chapter six

THE Marquis groaned as the ropes which had been very painfully constricting him were pulled away.

Then, when the burnous was taken off his head, he could still see nothing and realised he was in the darkness of a Bedouin tent.

He felt his coat being taken from him and the money from his pockets before he was left alone.

He had not attempted to struggle once he had been thrown down on the floor, realising it was useless and that there were men who could easily silence him with a blow.

Instead, he lay still, hoping they would think he was unconscious after the extremely unpleasant ride.

Only when he was quite certain that he was

alone did he sit up, rubbing first his arms back to circulation, then his legs.

He knew he was in an extremely dangerous position.

At the same time he guessed that he had been brought away by Bedouins, who would demand a very large ransom.

It had been impossible to keep from the people who lived around the Amphitheatre or anywhere in the neighbourhood the knowledge that he was a rich man who was paying for a large caravan.

The Bedouin robbers were known to be extremely avaricious where tourists were concerned.

Most of the Bedouins, who were all nomads moving from place to place, were honest and trustworthy, but, as in every society, there were always those who were the exact opposite.

The Marquis sat, getting back his breath.

The "swimming" feeling in his head which came from being tied up for such a long time was gradually receding.

He tried to remember all he had learned of the Bedouins in his previous trips to the East.

That they were very superstitious was something he had learned on other journeys.

Every man, woman, and child wore round their necks charms such as a porcupine's hand-shaped paw, since a hand, according to their ideas, was a most effective talisman against the "evil eye."

Apart from their superstitions, whatever the Bedouins did was done in the name of Allah, and scarcely a question was answered, or some action carried out without the exclamation "Allah be Praised."

Thinking back over the books he had bought to read about Tunisia, the Marquis guessed that the Bedouins who had captured him were the Suassi, who were known to live North of Djem.

It was a small tribe which obviously had aggressive members.

The Marquis thought he would know all the more when tomorrow he would be taken in front of their leader.

He was quite certain they would demand a very large ransom for him and he knew they would expect the money in cash.

The caravan would therefore have to proceed back to Tunis in order to obtain it.

The Marquis calculated that this might take five days or a week and with the same amount of time to return.

It was a horrifying thought, but he could see no way of shortening it, unless the head man in charge of the caravan had a large amount of money on him.

As this was extremely unlikely, he could only sit wondering frantically if there was any chance of escape.

Even while he was thinking of it the men who had left him, taking his coat and his money with them, came back.

As he heard them undoing the front of the tent, he lay down again and shut his eyes.

He then realised that he was not lying on the

sandy ground but on a mat, and that this, as long as he was in their power, would be his bed and the only thing he would have to sit on.

He knew that the nomads travelled with as few encumbrances as possible.

There would be nothing which was not considered a necessity and certainly no comforts by European standards.

Two men entered the tent which was so low that they had to bend their heads as they came towards the Marquis.

He did not look at them, but lay still and realised as they touched him that they were tying his feet together.

They then hammered a stout post into the ground beside him and they tied his hands to it.

He realised with dismay that he would be left for hours in an immobile position which would become intolerable during the heat of the day.

It would be, he knew, useless to protest.

He only hoped that when he saw the leader of his captors, he would be able to come to some terms which would not be so appallingly uncomfortable.

The two Bedouins had a lantern with them, but the Marquis deliberately did not open his eyes.

He guessed they were strong, broad-shouldered young men and it would be quite impossible for him to overpower two of them.

They did not speak the whole time they were tying him up, and they left the tent as silently as they had come, taking with them the lantern.

The Marquis reckoned from the length of time it had taken them to bring him and Kirkpatrick here on horseback that they were not more than a mile from El Djem.

He guessed that once the caravan had been sent in search of money for his ransom he would be taken much farther afield.

Perhaps he would be taken into the mountains, which would be a little nearer to Tunis.

This, however, was poor comfort unless he could think of some quicker way of arranging his escape.

He then remembered that he had told the Captain of his yacht to steam down the coast and wait for them at Mahdia, and there was every likelihood that he would be there by now.

Mahdia was a fishing-port perhaps thirty miles away.

He had thought that once they had seen the Amphitheatre and perhaps, although it was unlikely, found the treasure which Kirkpatrick insisted was there, it would be a bore to trek all the way back to Tunis.

This was something he had to arrange at the very beginning of their journey.

He had been informed that there was no chance of obtaining a good caravan with first-class camels and Arab horses except in Tunis.

The Marquis had also intended to have the very best tents which would certainly not be obtainable in any of the smaller towns in Tunisia.

Now he was calculating whether the Captain

would be able to supply him with the money which would be demanded.

It really rested, he knew, on how much the ransom asked and how valuable the Bedouins thought he was.

He lay still for about an hour.

Then his arms began to ache through being tied to the post, and he was aware the ropes around his feet were too tight and stopping the circulation of his blood.

He was not hungry, but he would have liked a drink, and he thought it was unlikely he would be given one.

The Bedouins would be crafty enough to think that if he were both hungry and thirsty in the morning, he would be all the more eager to agree to any ransom they demanded.

Too late the Marquis cursed himself and Kirkpatrick for not having taken with them a guard to ensure their safety while they were digging.

But he knew that would have revealed that they were looking for treasure and would also have made it impossible to keep anything they found a secret.

He might not be in his present predicament.

Although he was aware that Sabra must have seen them being carried off, he could not feel that made things any better.

She would, of course, alert the caravan as to what had happened.

He was certain that being concerned only for their animals, they would have no desire to arouse

128

the enmity of the Bedouins, or to take part in any dispute that ensued over the kidnapping.

"I have been a fool!" the Marquis told himself bitterly.

He remembered the revolver which he had actually brought with him on the journey, now lying in one of his cases.

But he had never envisaged it would be necessary for him to use it.

Outside the tent he could hear the chatter of voices.

The Bedouins would be sitting around the fire discussing what had happened and delighted to know that a rich man was in their power.

They had eaten, he thought, the usual dishes of little balls of mutton, cut-up eggs, and sheeps' cheese.

He had the uncomfortable feeling that that would be his only and inadequate diet for the next two weeks.

He would be thinking longingly of the excellent food which his chef provided on board the yacht and the even better food served in his Villa.

"Why was I so ridiculous as to agree to come on this damned trip?" he asked himself angrily.

There was no answer.

He had been mesmerised by Kirkpatrick into accepting a wild and very unlikely story of hidden treasure largely as a further excuse for running away from his responsibilities or what Sabra called "his duty."

Finally the chatter of voices outside had ceased and soon there was only silence.

The Marquis knew it must be growing late and he was sure that the stars would be coming out in the great arc of the sky overhead.

The Bedouins would all have gone into their black tents and be lying on their mats asleep.

Now was the only time when it would be possible to escape.

He tugged at the ropes which bound his hands, but he knew that however hard he tried, it would be impossible to free himself, and the same applied to his feet.

It was exasperating, infuriating, and he wanted to shout for help, but knew that none would be forthcoming.

He therefore tried to make himself as comfortable as he could and shut his eyes.

He was, in fact, tired, having lain awake so long the night before, thinking of Sabra.

That, however, was not something he wished to remember at the moment.

He told himself if he could get free, he would return immediately to France and make sure he never saw either Kirkpatrick or his daughter again.

Then in spite of his efforts not to—he found himself remembering the softness of Sabra's lips and the strange sensations she had aroused in him.

Although he hated to admit it, they were quite

different from anything he had ever felt for a woman before.

Frantically he tried to recall his father's strictures and his contempt for all women.

Instead, he could see Sabra's green and gold eyes under their wet lashes looking up at him.

He could see, too, the trembling of her lips just before he had kissed her.

He must have dozed off while he was thinking of her, for a slight sound awakened him and he had the unmistakable feeling that she was very near him.

He listened, aware that behind his head somebody was cutting the material of the tent.

He lay very still, wondering who it could be, and yet with his perception knowing who it was.

Then the tent was slit open and there was a faint light.

A moment later somebody crawled through the opening towards him and he knew it was Sabra.

He would have spoken to her if only in a whisper, but she put out her hand and laid it against his lips.

He felt a little thrill run through him almost as if she were kissing him.

Then her hands were on his arms and his feet and he guessed that she was feeling to see how he was fastened.

She moved away from him and he thought for one agonising moment that she was leaving him.

Then he realised she had not left the tent but

must have beckoned to someone outside, and then a moment later a man crawled in beside him.

Although he could not see his face, he knew it was Achmet.

He was a strong boy and with the same knife with which he had cut through the thick black material of which the tent was made, he then released the Marquis's arms and feet.

He sat up and Sabra put one hand on his shoulder, then with her head very close to his and her mouth against his ear, she whispered:

"You will have to . . . crawl away from here to where . . . we have . . . hidden the horses."

She would have moved away from him but the Marquis caught her by the shoulder to keep her from leaving his side and asked in a voice as low as hers:

"What about your father?"

"Papa is . . . dead," she replied. "He was . . . tied up as you were, but he has been . . . bitten by a . . . snake."

The Marquis was startled.

"Are you sure?"

"Quite sure . . . his body was already . . . cold and neither Achmet nor I could feel the . . . beat of his . . . heart."

There was a little pause before she added:

"You can look for yourself but it is . . . dangerous to . . . linger."

The Marquis knew this was true and he was sure that Sabra would not have said her father was dead if there was the slightest chance of his being alive.

At first he could hardly believe that anything so horrible could have happened.

As he turned to start crawling after her through the opening in the tent, he remembered that the snakes in Tunisia were very dangerous and a bite from some of them meant instant death.

As he moved out from the tent into the star-light, he saw that the Bedouins had pitched their camp on the edge of an orange grove.

There was only a little thin undergrowth, and he knew that Sabra had been right in saying they must move very carefully.

The only way in which they could avoid being seen was to crawl, as an Indian did, on their stom-achs.

As he lowered himself down on the ground, the Marquis realised that just a few feet away from his own tent was the one in which Kirkpatrick must have been imprisoned.

He could see the slit which Achmet had made to enter it.

He felt himself shiver as he thought it was not the Bedouins who had killed their prisoner, but what they would consider to be a direct instru-ment of Allah—a snake.

He found himself wondering whether they would encounter any more reptiles as they crawled slowly and as silently as possible away from the camp.

The Marquis's hands were severely scratched

by the prickly vegetation which he was aware even the horses disliked when they were being ridden in certain parts of the plain.

The spikes even penetrated his trousers, but there was nothing he could do except follow Sabra.

Achmet went ahead, taking the chance, the Marquis thought, of meeting a snake before it attacked them.

When one particularly thorny bramble had drawn blood from his fingers, the Marquis realised with relief that they were at last out of sight of the camp.

Just ahead of them, tied securely to some olive trees, were three horses.

With a sigh of relief Sabra rose to her feet, but she did not speak and, beckoning to the Marquis, ran light-footed until she reached them.

Achmet was there before her and she let him help her into the saddle before the Marquis could reach her.

Then, as he untied a horse which was the one he had ridden all the way from Tunis, Achmet leapt into the saddle of the third horse, and rode off.

The Marquis realised from the pace Sabra was setting that she was as frightened as he was that the Bedouins would discover their prisoner had escaped and follow them.

He knew the moon was not high but waning.

As he glanced at it, he remembered the prophecy of the fortune-teller that they would be in danger at the waning of the moon.

"I hate all these signs and portents!" he told himself petulantly. "The sooner I am away from this country, the better!"

There was, however, no point in saying so, and anyway, it was impossible because Sabra was ahead of him.

He thought after a little while that she was in fact making a wide detour to reach El Djem.

When at last they had left the Bedouin camp two miles behind them and there was no sign of their being followed, she drew in her horse and as the Marquis came alongside of her, she said:

"I have a plan, if you agree, that Achmet will return to the camp but say nothing of what has occurred tonight."

She paused a moment before she went on:

"He would, of course, have walked back if Papa had been with us, but now, with your permission, he will return on the horse he is riding."

She looked at the Marquis intently, as if she expected him to argue, but instead he asked:

"And where are we to go?"

"I heard you tell the Captain of your yacht to make for Mahdia and I think the sooner you are there, the safer you will be."

She drew in her breath before she said:

"It is unlikely that the Bedouins will follow us, but it would be a mistake to take any chances."

The Marquis smiled before he replied:

"I am in your hands."

Sabra drew a small bag from the pocket of her skirt and held it out towards him.

"I have brought with me the money you left hidden in your tent at El Djem. I have already remunerated generously on your behalf the man in charge of the caravan, but I thought you would wish to thank Achmet yourself."

She drew in her breath and went on:

"It was he who knew where the Bedouins were camped and I could not have managed to cut your bonds without him."

The Marquis took the money from her, realising she had been clever to find it.

Always when he travelled he hid his money by digging a hole in the ground and making sure it would not be discovered by petty theives.

He opened the bag and took out a large number of *francs*, in fact, so many that Achmet, when he received them, could only gasp his thanks.

Then Sabra held out her hand to the Berber boy, saying:

"Thank you from my heart! You have been more than kind and thanks be to Allah that you were there to help us."

Achmet's voice was very moving when he replied:

"*Marhabateu,*" which the Marquis knew meant "May Allah remain with you."

Then with a smile Sabra had turned away, riding confidently as if she knew her way to the sea.

It was a long ride and a tiring one.

Not only did the Marquis and Sabra flag before they came in sight of their destination, but so did the horses.

They stopped in a small, dirty village to water them, but there was nothing they could buy for themselves.

They rode on, picking small oranges from a tree which were easier to eat and more thirst-quenching than water, which was scarce and likely to be polluted.

When dawn broke, the Marquis could not help thinking that the first rays of the sun, which turned Sabra's hair to gold, were very beautiful.

He saw, too, in the daylight, that she was very pale.

He knew she must be suffering from the shock of finding her father dead as well as the unhappiness of losing him.

Because she still seemed to think it was imperative that they should move as quickly as possible, the Marquis did not feel that now was the time to speak of Kirkpatrick.

Instead, he concentrated on getting himself and Sabra out of danger.

He was praying that the Captain of his yacht had obeyed his instructions, for if he had done so, he should be in Mahdia by now.

It would be an incalculable relief to be aboard *The Mermaid* again.

Long before the sea came into view, there was a cool breeze blowing from it over the sun-drenched earth, and there was the taste of salt in the air.

Then at last they could see in the distance the brilliant blue of the Mediterranean under an equally blue sky and ships silhouetted against it.

Now there were people, camels, mules, and sheep, the women walking bare-footed behind their husbands, who rode in comfort.

Other women were completely enveloped in burnouses, veils, and yashmaks.

Small boys dodged in and out of the passers-by and held out pleading hands to the Marquis and Sabra as they rode on.

Then, as if it had materialised out of the sea itself, there was the harbour built on a promontory, with boats coming and going in and out of the small port as they had done for many hundreds of years.

As they rode onto the promontory, the Marquis remembered that Mahdia had once been a lair for an infamous pirate called Dragut.

He was a Corsair who made it his base for many raids on Malta, and on one occasion he had kidnapped almost the whole population of Gozo and sold them in slave-markets.

Even to think of kidnapping made the Marquis shudder, and he wondered how he could ever be sufficiently grateful to Sabra for saving him.

Then with an inexpressible joy he saw in the best position in the fishing port lay the sleek lines of *The Mermaid*.

Sabra saw her at the same time as he did, and

she spoke for the first time for over an hour as she said:

"We have . . . done it! We have got here! Now, My Lord . . . you . . . are safe!"

The Marquis was about to reply, "And so are you!" when she hurried her tired horse down the twisting road which led to the Quay.

As they dismounted in front of the yacht, two seamen, recognising the Marquis, hurried to their horses' heads.

It took time for the Marquis to give instructions as to what was to be done about the horses.

He arranged for them to be kept until they could be collected by the owner of the caravan, while Sabra disappeared into the yacht.

He thought she wanted to wash away the dust of their ride and he wished to do the same thing.

The Marquis went aboard to find there was a bath ready for him and some clean clothes that he had left in his Stateroom.

He was not surprised when he entered the Saloon to find not only luncheon, which he had ordered, waiting for him, but also Sabra.

He realised she was wearing the same clothes in which she had ridden to the yacht, but he saw that she had washed her hair.

It was shining like a halo round her head as it framed her small face and huge eyes.

"I am sure you are very hungry," the Marquis remarked, "as I am."

"At the moment it is . . . difficult to think of anything but that you are . . . safe."

There was a note in her voice which told the Marquis all too clearly how worried she had been and how much it had meant to her.

He thought it would be a mistake until they had eaten and relaxed to talk of her father's death or discuss the future.

Instead, he gave her a glass of champagne and drank one himself.

Then, as the food arrived, they sat down at the table, the Marquis thinking of the distasteful Arab food dishes he had feared he would have to eat for so long while he was a prisoner.

Because Sabra was really as hungry as he was, they ate in silence.

When coffee had been served and the Marquis had accepted a glass of brandy, he sat back comfortably in his armchair, and, crossing his legs, said:

"I am wondering, Sabra, how I can adequately express my gratitude for your brilliance and your courage in getting me away from what would have been an extremely uncomfortable prison, if nothing else."

She did not answer and he went on:

"You know that I am very sorry about your father!"

There was a little silence, then Sabra said:

"I was thinking as we were riding here that perhaps it was . . . best . . . for him."

"To die?" the Marquis questioned.

"He was finding it more and more difficult to live," Sabra said, "and when you took pity on us, he had only a few *francs* left."

The Marquis looked at her for a moment before he said:

"And yet you tried to dissuade him from approaching me and appeared not to approve of his suggestion that we should go in search of hidden treasure."

Sabra did not answer, and he said:

"What had you against me?"

Again she did not reply, and he thought perhaps it was a mistake to bother her with questions at this particular moment.

Instead, he bent forward across the table, and, putting out his hand palm upwards, said:

"Listen to me, Sabra, I realise you are now alone in the world, but I promise you I will look after you and protect you. You will be my responsibility from now on."

His voice was very low and deep, and almost as if she found it impossible to ignore his outstretched hand, very slowly Sabra put her fingers in his.

His hand tightened and he said:

"I want you to be happy, and if you will stop fighting me and let me do as I say and look after you, then I am sure I can make you happy."

His voice was very beguiling, and as she raised her eyes to look into his, there was a sudden radiance on her face as there had been the previous night when he had kissed her.

He held her hand very closely as he said:

"I do not want to talk to you about your father for the moment, or even about you. I therefore suggest, as we are both very tired, that you go to your cabin and sleep."

He gave a short laugh as he went on:

"It has been a long night, in fact, the longest and most gruelling night I can ever remember. But it is entirely due to you, Sabra, that we are here, and now you need never be afraid again!"

Her fingers were fluttering in his at what he had said.

He thought as she just looked at him that her eyes, very large and seeming to hold the sunshine, made her more beautiful than anyone he had ever seen in his life before.

He wanted to kiss her lips, but they were in the Saloon and at any moment the stewards might come in to collect the dishes.

He therefore just raised her hand to his lips.

"Go to bed, Sabra," he said. "We are leaving here immediately and when you are rested, we have a great many things to discuss together."

The colour had risen in her cheeks when he had kissed her hand.

Now she just gave him a smile, which made her look even more lovely, although he was aware that her lips were trembling a little.

He thought, too, there was a suspicion of tears in her eyes.

She went from the Saloon, moving quickly and with a grace that was undeniable.

Seeing her golden hair vanish as she closed the door, he thought how different she would look when he had dressed her in clothes that would enhance rather than detract from her beauty.

Anywhere, even in Marlborough House or Buckingham Palace, she would outshine all the beauties who were so fulsomely acclaimed in the Women's Magazines and in the newspapers.

"She is certainly very different from anybody I have every met before," the Marquis told himself.

Then, like a spectre at the feast, was the problem in his mind as to how he could possibly marry the daughter of Michael Kirkpatrick.

The Marquis would have been obtuse, which he was not, if he was not aware of what manner of man Kirkpatrick was.

Without his calculated charm and his mesmeric skill in drawing golden guineas from the pockets of men who listened to him, he and Sabra would have starved.

After all, although he had run away from it, the Marquis was vividly aware of the importance of Quin and of his Social position.

However reluctant he might be to accept his responsibilities, he now had to return to England, where the Marquess of Salisbury and all his relations were expecting him to take his place at Court.

He must also take his place in the County, which was something he could not evade.

How could Sabra, however intelligent she

might be, understand what it would entail to be his wife and the mistress of his houses?

How could she entertain as she would be expected to do, not only at Quin, but also the Statesmen, the Politicians, and the Royalty who had always enjoyed the hospitality of Quin House in Park Lane?

"I will look after her; she can have anything in the world she wants," the Marquis murmured.

But even as he protested to himself, he knew that Sabra would accept nothing from him unless she had the justification—to put it quite simply—of being his wife.

He rose from the chair in which he had been sitting, to walk across the Saloon out on deck.

The yacht had moved from the port while they were eating their luncheon.

Already they were leaving the coast and would soon be out to sea, heading as quickly as possible for Nice.

"When we get there," the Marquis told himself, "I must talk to Sabra and make her understand."

Then he was not so confident, knowing in his heart that it would be a waste of time, for she would not listen.

He walked along the deck and stood in the bow.

Ahead was the horizon, where the sea touched the sky.

He remembered how he had looked at the horizon once before from his Villa, when he was wondering whether he would go South or North.

Then Kirkpatrick had made the decision for him and he had gone South.

There had been no treasure, or at least he had not found it, but there was Sabra.

After all they had been through together, and vibrations he had felt between them, he could not let her walk out of his life in the same manner in which she had come into it.

When he kissed her, it had been an instinctive act without thought.

After that she had saved him from being imprisoned by the Bedouins.

Perhaps even from dying, as her father had died, before he could be rescued or pay the ransom which he knew would be demanded.

And before that any number of things might have happened.

The Arabs were not always kind to their prisoners, and they would not understand how hardships which would seem quite ordinary to them would be almost intolerable to a man brought up to a different way of life.

"She saved me!" the Marquis said softly.

He thought how clever she had been to arrange for the caravan to return to Tunis, where the money the Marquis had promised would be waiting for them.

She had also brought away the bag of money he had hidden, having found it where no other woman he could think of would have known where to look.

He wanted to ask her whether she had used her intuition rather than her mind.

He wanted to know a great deal about her life before he had met her.

It struck him that while Kirkpatrick had talked unceasingly to make him laugh and keep him amused, he had never been at all revealing about himself or where he had come from, and had seldom spoken of his wife.

"The whole thing is ridiculously mysterious!" the Marquis said angrily.

Once again he was trying to visualise Sabra at Quin, coping with his dull but very critical Bourne relatives.

They considered themselves the equals, if not the superiors, of everybody else in the Social World, and seldom allowed strangers to forget it.

How could Sabra possibly, after living such a sordid life with her father, cope with that?

"I must talk to her," the Marquis said to himself, and was even more certain than he was already that it would be to no avail.

She loved him, he knew that, and he had the feeling, and it made him anxious, that she had never loved anybody else in the same way.

But was love enough?

Would love not disintegrate, as his father had always said it would, into boredom, indifference, contempt, or, perhaps, on her part, unfaithfulness?

She might leave him as his mother had left his father.

"Oh, God, what can I do?" the Marquis asked the waves washing against the sides of the yacht.

He wanted Sabra, he could feel his whole body vibrating towards her.

At the same time he was afraid, desperately afraid.

If he broke his vow to have nothing to do with women, it might be something he would bitterly regret.

Then his father would have been right when he had taught him that women were the devil, to be avoided at all costs.

chapter seven

ON reaching her cabin, exhaustion had swept over
Sabra like a tidal wave.

She could no longer think, she could no longer
even be elated that she had stolen the Marquis
away from his kidnappers.

All she wanted to do was to sleep.

When she was shown into her cabin by the
steward who had looked after her on the outward
journey, he asked:

"Is there anything I can get you, Miss?"

"No, thank you," Sabra replied.

She found there was a can of warm water for
her to wash with.

She pulled off her clothes which were dirty
from the sand and the undergrowth through which
she had crawled to save the Marquis.

They had also been torn in places by the prickly brambles and the cacti.

She wondered vaguely how she could wear them tomorrow.

Then she could think of nothing else but the comfort of the bed which was waiting for her.

She had no nightgown and she crept between the sheets naked. As her head touched the pillow she fell asleep.

It became rough not long after they headed out to sea to make for Nice, but Sabra had no idea of it.

"Is Miss Kirkpatrick still asleep?" the Marquis asked the steward who was valeting him.

"Fast asleep, M'Lord! If Your Lordship asks me, 'tis the best thing that can 'appen to the young lady."

"I agree with you," the Marquis said.

After dinner the next evening, however, when the whole day had passed without a sound from Sabra, he thought it wise to see for himself.

He therefore went down to her cabin, opened the door very quietly, and in the light from the passageway he could see her clearly.

Her head was turned against the pillow, and her golden hair was vivid against the whiteness of the linen.

He drew nearer, and, as his eyes became accustomed to the half-darkness, he could see that she was utterly relaxed and deeply asleep, like a child who is not even dreaming.

She looked very young and her eye-lashes were dark against her cheeks.

He thought, too, that she was very lovely, so lovely that he could never remember seeing a woman look more beautiful when she was sleeping.

As he had thought before, she was more like a young goddess than a human girl.

As he stood beside the bed looking down at her, it was as if his vibrations touched hers.

She moved a little restlessly, turning over on her other side.

As she did so, the Marquis had a glimpse of an exquisite rosy-tipped white breast.

He realised that in fact he was looking at somebody who was very human and very much a woman.

Then he knew she was the women he wanted, and could not lose, but he still did not know how he could keep her in his life.

He stood for a long time looking down at her, aware that the blood was throbbing in his temples.

He wanted more than he had ever wanted anything before to put out his hands to touch her.

Then, as quietly as he had entered the cabin, he went from it, closing the door behind him.

The yacht was in sight of the coast of France and steaming towards Nice harbour early the next morning.

A steward brought the Marquis his hot shaving

water and put out the clothes he would wear that day.

"Miss Kirkpatrick's awake, M'Lord," he said conversationally.

"Awake?" the Marquis questioned. "Have you taken her something to eat?"

" 'Course, M'Lord!" the Steward replied with a note of reproach in his voice that the Marquis had thought him so lacking in his duty.

He continued:

"The young lady ate a good breakfast and, I think, M'Lord, as her means leavin' us when we reaches harbour."

The Marquis was very still. Then he asked:

"Why should you think that?"

"She was enquirin', M'Lord, about the trains to Calais and wot would be the price of the cheapest ticket."

The Marquis did not speak, and the steward went on:

"I was just wonderin', M'Lord, if the young lady left any clothes at the Villa afore we set out on this trip."

He paused a moment before he went on:

"I've done me best with wot she was a-wearin', but the skirt of 'er dress is in a terrible state—terrible!"

Still the Marquis did not speak.

He went to the porthole, looked at the sunshine bathing the hotels and Villas on the coast in gold, and reckoned they would anchor within the next hour.

He stood for a while staring, as if he had never seen the coast of France before. Then he asked:

"Have you removed Miss Kirkpatrick's breakfast-tray?"

"I was intendin' doin' that when Your Lordship no longer needed me."

"Do it now," the Marquis ordered, "and bring me her dress if it is in her cabin!"

The steward looked surprised before he said:

"As it 'appens, M'Lord, it's still dryin' after I washed it, but I thinks now as it'd be all right for 'er to wear it."

"Bring it to me!" the Marquis ordered.

Sabra had finished her breakfast and as the tray was collected from her cabin by the steward she asked him:

"How soon shall we be arriving?"

"In about twenty minutes, Miss, and 'Is Lordship's goin' ashore soon as we ties up alongside."

Sabra did not say anything.

This was what she had wanted to know, and once the Marquis had gone, she would be able to make her escape.

She had thought it over earlier.

She awoke while it was still dark, although the first glimpse of the sun was a golden bar on the horizon.

She had known then that she had to leave the Marquis because she loved him too much to accept what he clearly had in mind.

He had said that he would look after her, and she would never "want for anything."

He used almost the same words she had heard from the men from whom her father was extracting money.

That was when she decided to disguise herself.

Wearing tinted spectacles, she made sure that from the moment of their acquaintance they realised she wished to avoid them.

Because her spectacled face made her very different from the girl with the golden hair and green eyes, she had, in fact, received no further invitations to become some man's mistress.

She had never imagined for one moment when they set out for Tunisia that the Marquis would offer the same position in his life that other men had suggested in the past.

"I love him, Mama," she said in her heart to her mother. "How can I do anything so wrong or so wicked...even though I expect Papa would think it advantageous...just because he is...so rich."

Then as if it were an agony even to think of such things, she put her hands over face.

She did not cry: she knew that would come later when she had left *The Mermaid* for ever and would never see him again.

Now she asked herself bitterly why out of all the men in the world did she have to fall in love with a man who was so important.

She knew he would not contemplate for one

moment making the daughter of Michael Kirkpatrick his wife.

She loved him to much to accept the degradation of what he was prepared to offer her.

It was then she made up her mind that nothing would induce her to go back to the Villa.

She would not argue with him on a subject which would only be embarrassing for both of them.

She decided what she must do, but the only difficulty was to have enough money to enable her to reach England.

She thought of the bag of coins she had discovered in the Marquis's tent at El Djem.

He had buried it cleverly but not so cleverly that she could not find it.

It would have been easy for her to extract, before she handed it back to him, what she needed.

But that would be stealing, even though she needed the money not only to save herself, but also him.

She therefore decided that as soon as the Marquis had gone ashore, she would ask the Captain to lend her what she required for the journey, saying she intended to go shopping.

She knew that the Marquis would refund the money to the Captain when he was aware of it.

She was sure, therefore, there would be no difficulties.

She would also return every penny she borrowed as soon as possible to the Marquis so that she would no longer be in his debt.

Having made her decision, and realising she would need some sort of conveyance to take her to the station, she got out of bed.

Having washed, she started to dress herself.

She found her underclothes and realised they had been carefully washed and pressed while she was asleep.

She supposed it was the Steward who had done this, and she wished she could tip him before she left the yacht.

She knew, however, she would need every penny she could obtain from the Captain to get her back to England.

When she was dressed, except for her gown, she sat down in front of the mirror which was attached to the wall to arrange her hair.

After all she had been through she was rather short of hairpins.

Somehow she managed to twist her long tresses around her small head and pin them neatly into place.

She realised that not only her gown, but also her broad-brimmed hat that she had remembered to bring with her from El Djem was battered and worn.

But actually her hat, which she had left attached to the saddle of her horse, was in better shape than her gown in which she had crawled to and from the Bedouin camp.

Only to think of it made her remember how frightened she had been that she might be discovered before she could reach her father and the Marquis.

Her heart had beaten frantically as she had crawled through the grass and felt the prickly brambles and cacti scratching at her hands and legs and tearing at her skirt.

Then when she reached the first tent and Achmet slit it open she had found her father dead.

At first she had thought it strange that he was lying so still and silent.

When she touched him, his hands and his face were cold.

It was Achmet who had realised it was a snake-bite that had killed him and there was nothing they could do for him.

She had then crawled to the next tent, where she had found the Marquis.

She had been desperately afraid that he, too, might be dead.

Sabra could still feel the leap of her heart when she knew he was about to speak.

Terrified he might be overheard by the Bedouins, she had put her fingers to his lips.

To think of his lips now and the way he had kissed her in the Amphitheatre made her tremble.

Hurriedly, she turned from the mirror, thinking she should not waste time but must be ready to leave the yacht as soon as the Marquis had gone ashore.

She heard the engines stop and was aware they had drawn up alongside the Quay, and the gang-plank was being let down.

It was then she opened the cupboard in her cabin, where her gown should be hanging.

When she had taken it off, she had thrown it down on a chair with the rest of her clothes on top of it.

She had been too tired for sleep.

Now she looked into the cupboard to find it was empty.

She realised the Steward must have taken her gown to wash it, and she went back to the bedside and tugged at the bell-pull.

She guessed it was connected with a bell that could be heard at the other end of the yacht and was sure the Steward would come immediately.

She sat down on the side of the bed to wait.

Then, feeling embarrassed because she was wearing only her bodice and her shoulders were bare, she draped a Turkish towel over herself and sat down again.

To her surprise, however, no one came, and after a moment she rose to her feet and went to the door.

She thought perhaps she was receiving no attention because everybody was concerned with their arrival in the port.

The only thing she could do would be to call out and hope that either her own Steward or one of the others would hear her.

She turned the handle of the door, thought it was stuck, and pulled it harder.

It was then she realised she had been locked in.

More than two hours passed before sitting waiting on her bed Sabra heard the key turn in the lock.

There was a knock on the door, and without waiting for a reply it opened.

It was the Steward who came in carrying a large dress-box in one hand and a hat-box in the other.

He put them both down on the bed beside Sabra and said:

"I'm sorry if you've bin waitin', Miss, but 'Is Lordship took me wiv 'im to buy you somethin' decent to wear. I couldn't do a thing with your own gown, an' that's the truth!"

"The Marquis has been buying me clothes?" Sabra exclaimed.

It seemed stupid now not to think that was what he would be doing.

"We couldn't 'ave you goin' ashore lookin' like a scarecrow, Miss, now could we?" The Steward grinned. "An' I thinks you'll look a treat in wot 'Is Lordship's chosen for you."

He opened the cardboard box, undid the tapes which kept the tissue paper smooth over what lay beneath it, then said:

"I'll wait outside, Miss, while you puts it on, then if you'll give me a call, I'll come back an' button it up for you."

He paused just a second before he continued:

"It's not the sort of gown you'll be able to manage on your own, I can tell you that!"

Without waiting for her reply, he grinned at

her again, then went from the cabin, closing the door behind him.

For a moment Sabra just sat staring at what lay in the cardboard box.

She felt it was something she should refuse, as she had refused so many other offers from the Marquis.

Now it would be impossible for her to do so.

Her own gown had been taken away from her, and she could hardly walk about dressed in petticoats with only a Turkish towel to cover her naked shoulders.

Slowly, wanting to fight the Marquis but knowing that she would be unable to do so, she lifted the gown he had bought for her from its box.

It was very pretty, and she knew also that it was expensive and in exceedingly good taste.

It was a gown her mother would have admired.

Designed for a young girl, yet it had the unmistakable *chic* which only the French can achieve where women's clothes are concerned.

It was simple and yet amazingly elegant, trimmed with broderie anglaise.

Sabra was to find when she opened the hat-box that there was a hat of the same material which was trimmed with white flowers and satin ribbons.

When she had put on her gown she could only stare at her reflection in the mirror.

Then she called the steward and he deftly fastened her up the back.

"Now, Miss," he said, "you look as you ought

to, so to speak, and very pretty, too, if I may say so!"

"Thank you."

Sabra looked once again into the mirror.

"I . . . I think it is . . . how my mother would . . . want me to look," she said softly.

"I'm sure that's the truth, Miss," the Steward agreed with a smile. "An' that's 'ow 'Is Lordship wants you to look too. 'E's waitin' for you outside in a carriage."

Just for one moment Sabra thought she should defy him and refuse to join him.

Then she knew she had no choice in the matter.

"Thank you for looking after me," she said to the Steward. "I am very grateful to you."

"It's bin a pleasure, Miss." He smiled and opened the door for her.

She walked slowly up the companionway and out onto the deck.

The Captain was waiting beside the gang-plank to shake her by the hand and she knew as she saw the expression in his eyes that he admired her.

As she walked away she saw the Marquis step out of an open carriage to stand on the Quay waiting until she reached him.

She could not speak but only got into the carriage, and as the Marquis joined her, the horses moved off.

He turned a little sideways with his arm across the back of her seat to look at her.

She was acutely conscious of him even while

she pretended to be staring at the view on the other side of the carriage.

Then, as the horses increased their pace, Sabra was aware that soon they would be climbing up the road which led to the Top Corniche.

She said as if the words were drawn from her:

"I . . . I suppose I should say . . . thank you for . . . my . . . gown and my . . . hat."

"You have thanked me already by looking just as I wanted you to," the Marquis replied.

"I . . . wanted to wear my own gown," Sabra flashed at him.

"If you have seen the mess it was in, you would realise it was fit only for the rubbish-bin."

"At least it was mine!"

"So is what you are wearing now," the Marquis retorted. "You must learn, Sabra, to accept presents graciously, because I like giving them to you."

Sabra drew in her breath, realising what he implied.

But she felt this was not the moment to start an argument, when it was impossible for her to escape.

They drove on in silence until there was the sight of the trees, the white Villas, and the breath-taking view below them of the Mediterranean.

Despite herself, Sabra felt the loveliness of it lift her whole being.

She knew in the garden below it there would be bougainvillaea, hybiscus, and climbing geraniums, and even to think of them was like coming home.

Determinedly she told herself she must not weaken.

She must tell the Marquis once and for all that she was leaving him and that nothing he could say or do would stop her.

The servants greeted them at the door of the Villa and they walked into the cool of the room which opened onto the verandah.

Sabra thought it looked even more beautiful than when she had last seen it.

She loved the serenity of the Villa, the white rugs on the floor, the soft cushions, and the pictures which she was aware were all by great artists and very valuable.

"Let me give you a glass of champagne," the Marquis said quietly.

They were the first words he had spoken since they had discussed her gown.

"No . . . thank you."

"I think at least you should drink to our happiness," he said, "which is something about which I wish to talk to you."

Without thinking, she pulled her hat from her head and threw it down in one of the chairs.

The Marquis put a glass of champagne within her reach and held another in his own hand. Then he said:

"You are looking as I always wanted you to, without those disfiguring spectacles, and very different from how you looked the last time you were here."

"I hope you will give them back to me, for I would not wish to travel back to England . . . alone without . . . them."

"So you are going to England?"

"Yes."

"Since that is where I have to go too, as you have pointed out to me so often, surely we can go there together?"

There was a note in his voice that made Sabra's heart turn over in her breast.

She dared not look at him for fear he would see the love in her eyes.

She could think of nothing more wonderful than that they should go back to England together.

Then she told herself she had to be strong.

She must not listen to the weakness which made her long to run towards him and lift her lips to his.

"Are you really intending to leave me, Sabra?" the Marquis asked gently.

"I . . . I have to . . . you must . . . understand . . . I have to!"

"Why?"

"Because I cannot . . . do as you ask . . . I have to be true to what I believe is right . . . not only for myself . . . but also for . . . you."

"So you are thinking of me!"

"Of course . . . I am thinking of . . . you. You have a . . . great position and you are of . . .

importance not only in yourself and your family but... also to England and The... Queen. You should not... besmirch that position with me."

"That is something I have no intention of doing," the Marquis said firmly.

"Then you... understand... why I must... leave you."

"I do not understand, and as far as I am concerned, it would be the worst thing that could happen to me."

Because he spoke so positively, Sabra looked at him in surprise and he said very softly:

"I think, my darling, you are being very foolish for the first time since I have known you, and very obtuse."

He paused, then as Sabra did not speak, he went on:

"Up to now, you have always used your perception, and yet, when it is most important you should use it, it appears to have failed you."

"I... I do not know... what you... m-mean."

Sabra's voice was only a whisper, and it seemed somehow stifled in her throat.

"I mean, my precious," the Marquis said, "that we are going to be married this afternoon!"

He paused to give emphasis to his words.

"If you will allow me first a few days honeymoon, we will then go back to England and face the music," he continued.

"M-married?" Sabra could hardly say the word.

Then as the Marquis started towards her she said:

"No, no . . . of course not . . . how can you think of marrying me after . . . Papa's scheme to . . . take so much . . . money . . . from . . ."

She stopped because it was impossible to control her voice.

Then the Marquis's arms were around her.

She looked up at him desperately and he said:

"Your father no longer matters, nothing matters, my precious, except that I want you and I have no intention of losing you!"

Then his lips came down on hers.

While she knew somewhere at the back of her mind she should resist him, she felt herself go limp in his arms and her whole body merged into his.

Then as he kissed her and went on kissing her there was nothing else in the world but him.

The Marquis raised his head.

"How can you make me feel like this?" he asked. "God, how I love you!"

Then he was kissing her again.

He kissed her until Sabra felt if only she could die now she would have touched the very zenith of love and nothing else could ever be so wonderful.

Yet she knew she wanted to live—live for the Marquis—although because she loved him she should prevent him from making a mistake.

Once again he was looking down at her.

"I want you to tell me what you feel about me," he said. "You have fought me for long enough."

"I . . . I love . . . you!" Sabra said in a broken little voice. "I love you . . . so that you are the sea
. . . the sky . . . the whole world . . . there is nothing
else . . . but you . . . but you should not . . . marry
me."

"You are mine!" the Marquis said fiercely. "And
if you think I can live without you, or do any of
the things you want me to do without you, then
you are very much mistaken!"

His lips twisted in a mocking smile as he said:

"If you will not marry me, then I will go
straight back to El Djem and look for that elusive
treasure."

He stopped talking to smile at her before he
continued:

"If I am captured again by the Bedouins, you
will have to come out and rescue me again."

"How can you say . . . anything so . . . crazy?"
Sabra asked.

"The alternative is quite simple," he said. "You
will do your duty as my wife and look after me,
and doubtless you will make me do a million
things I have no wish to do, but it will be better
than being useless and empty-handed without
you."

Sabra gave a little choked laugh.

"How can . . . you even think . . . such things!"

He drew her a little closer as he said:

"Everything will be quite simple, my precious,
if you will leave it to me."

He paused a moment before he went on:

"I knew when I saw you singing to the children that you were everything I wanted as my wife, but I was afraid, desperately afraid of making a mistake where a woman was concerned."

"How are you so... certain you are not... making a mistake now?" Sabra asked.

"As soon as I learnt you were planning to leave me," the Marquis replied. "I knew that my life would be totally worthless and I would be miserable, utterly miserable, without you."

He gave a short laugh as he said:

"There is no need for me to explain what I felt in words..."

He stopped speaking for a moment before he continued:

"I can read your thoughts and you can read mine, and you know only too clearly that we both need each other and how unhappy we will be unless we are together."

"That is... true," Sabra whispered, "but..."

"There are no 'buts,'" the Marquis said firmly. "You are mine, and when we are married, my lovely one, I will make you love me as much as I love you."

He looked at her face before he said:

"When I saw you asleep, it was with a superhuman effort that I did not kiss you back to wakefulness and tell you how perfect you are in every way."

"How can you... say anything so... marvellous to... me?" Sabra asked. "I have been... so mi-

168

serable and . . . unhappy for . . . so long that I cannot believe . . . what I am . . . feeling now . . . or that I can be . . . your wife."

She hesitated, then she asked like a child wanting to be reassured:

"You do really . . . mean that we are to be . . . married?"

"We are being married at two-thirty," the Marquis said. "We have first to go to the *mairie*, which is obligatory in France, and be married by the Mayor."

He paused a moment before he went on:

"Then I have arranged that our wedding service will take place in the British Church in Nice, where a Clergyman will be waiting for us."

He kissed her again before he said:

"Before I go on telling you how much you mean to me, we must fill in this form and send it to the Mayor. The carriage is waiting to take it to him, and we have to give him the particulars which the French require."

With his arm around Sabra's waist, he drew her across the room to where there was a table in front of a sofa.

They sat down side-by-side, and the Marquis kept one arm around her as he took a form from an inside pocket and put it on the table in front of him.

Sabra saw that his names were already filled in and learned for the first time that they were

Victor William Mark, 7th Marquis of Quin-bourne.

Beneath this was a space for her own name.

"Sabra Mary," she said before the Marquis could ask her.

He wrote it down then filled in her father's name.

Michael Kirkpatrick.

"And now your mother's," he said.

There was a distinct pause before in what was a very low, hesitating little voice, Sabra replied:

"E... Elizabeth... Mary... Bourne."

The Marquis looked at her in astonishment.

"Bourne?" he questioned. "You are a relation of mine?"

She looked away from him and he saw the colour rise in her cheeks.

"That is the... reason why I did not... wish Papa to... approach you... and why we knew so much... about... you."

"Why did you not tell me?"

"I was... ashamed... and besides... Mama was an... outcast from your family."

"I do not understand."

"She... ran away with Papa... she was very young and you can imagine how persuasive he was and how... fascinating he seemed to a... young girl."

The Marquis knew exactly what she was saying, and after a moment he asked:

"Who is your grandfather?"

"He is now the Lord Chancellor, Viscount Bourne, a first cousin of the late . . . Marquis."

"I can hardly believe it!" the Marquis exclaimed. "Then your mother was the Honourable Elizabeth Bourne!"

"Yes . . . but Grandpapa was not made a Viscount until after she had run away with Papa and although Papa wanted her to use her title, she would not do so."

She gave a little sob.

"Her father was so furious at her marrying Papa that neither he nor her . . . family would have anything . . . further to do . . . with her."

The Marquis was listening, but he did not speak, and after a moment Sabra continued:

"Mama had a little . . . money of her . . . own. It was only two hundred pounds a year, but it was enough for us to live in a . . . cottage in the country . . . where we were . . . very happy until . . . she died."

She drew in her breath as if she could hardly bear to think of it. Then she went on:

"Sometimes Papa was restless . . . but he was happy too . . . until he had no money at all."

"You mean your mother's allowance died with her?" the Marquis asked.

"It was a legacy from her mother, but it could be inherited only by a son . . . if she had . . . one."

There was a pain in Sabra's voice which told the

Marquis all too clearly how much she regretted that she had been born a girl rather than a boy.

He pulled her closer to him as he said:

"I am very, very glad, my precious, that your mother had a daughter, but I can hardly believe what you are telling me."

"It was all so . . . horrible after . . . Mama died," Sabra whispered. "Papa had no way of making money . . . except that he was . . . amusing and witty."

She shook her head as she remembered, before she went on:

"The men we met as we wandered about the world were ready to . . . pay him to keep them . . . laughing."

"That was no sort of life for you!" the Marquis declared.

"It got worse and worse as I grew . . . older," Sabra whispered, "and Papa . . . wanted me to . . . help him . . . but I knew it was . . . something Mama would not approve of . . . and when I refused he was very . . . angry."

The Marquis's lips tightened, but he did not say anything.

"It got more horrible," Sabra want on, "because Papa's reputation began to spread and people would warn a . . . man before he could . . . approach him."

She hid her face against him and continued:

"Then when Papa insisted on coming to see you, he had nothing left but . . . I still . . . tried to . . . stop him."

"Thank God he was sensible enough to do what he wished, rather than listen to you," the Marquis said. "Supposing I had never met you, supposing I had never found you?"

He pulled her closer and almost roughly into his arms.

Then he was kissing her demandingly, fiercely, aggressively, but she was not afraid.

She only knew that her mother had looked after her.

Although she had never expected it, she had stepped back into her mother's world.

What she had suffered with her father could be forgotten.

Only when they knelt in front of the Parson in the small empty British Church and he blessed them did Sabra really believe that as the Marquis's wife she was safe for ever and need never be afraid again.

When they had pulled back the curtains so that lying in bed they could see the stars, Sabra whispered:

"How could I have ... guessed ... how could I have ... imagined for one moment when you ... kissed me in the Amphitheatre?"

She paused for a moment before whispering:

"When you lifted me up to the ... stars that those same stars would be shining down on us now?"

"They are the stars of love," the Marquis said,

"and you are to forget everything that has frightened you and made you unhappy until now."

He pulled her a little closer as he asked:

"I have made you happy, my lovely darling?"

It was a question and she replied, and the answer came from the very depths of her soul:

"I...did not know that...such happiness... existed."

"Nor did I," he said gently, "and, my adorable one, I believe now that Fate has ruled our lives and brought us together after we have known each other in other lives."

The Marquis gave her a tender smile before he continued:

"Perhaps—who knows?—on other journeys, and whatever happens we can never now be separated."

"I...I believe that...too," Sabra said, "and our lives are...eternal and there is nothing... greater than love or more Divine!"

The Marquis drew in his breath.

"I have been so desperately afraid of marrying a woman who would be all the things my father warned me against, but now I know, my darling, that you are part of me."

He gave her a quick kiss before he went on:

"Without you I am incomplete. So we will find happiness together: a happiness we must never lose!"

"I will never let you...lose it," Sabra said, "and I think our...perception...which is very acute...will warn us of obstacles and...

difficulties so that we can ... overcome them long before they become ... dangerous in any way."

The Marquis laughed. Then he said:

"I cannot believe anything could be more dangerous physically than what we have encountered already. At the same time, my perfect little wife, there is so much that is Spiritual which you have to teach me."

He spoke seriously, and Sabra said:

"I think you are ... wonderful ... everything about you is ... wonderful and the only ... thing that makes me ... afraid is that I might ... fail you."

"How could you possibly do that?" he asked. "It is far more likely that I shall fail in what you call my 'duty,' which quite frankly has terrified me until now."

"I do not think you need be ... frightened of anything!" Sabra said. "But ... can I tell you what I want ... more than anything ... else in the ... world?"

"Whatever it is, I will give it to you, my darling, even if it means tearing down the stars from the sky."

There was a note in the Marquis's voice which told her how much he loved her, and he felt her body quiver against his before she said:

"What I want ... and what I think you need too is ... a home. I have missed my home since Mama died. I have always dreamt ... of having a tiny ... cottage where I would be with ... somebody I loved ... as much as I love ... you."

175

"No one could describe Quin as a 'tiny cottage,' " the Marquis said, "but does it really matter where we are so long as we are together?"

"No . . . of course not," Sabra answered. "I will make it a . . . home for you even if it is as large as the Amphitheatre at El Djem. All that matters is that . . . you and I are there . . . and in time . . . our children."

He could hardly hear the last two words, but her shyness and the way she spoke made the fire come into the Marquis's eyes.

He turned towards her, and his lips were very close to hers as he said:

"I want to see my son in your arms and hear you sing to him as you sang 'All Things Bright and Beautiful' to the Arab children."

He paused before he went on:

"That, my precious, is what I will give you, because everything around you should be beautiful."

"It will . . . be," Sabra said simply, "if . . . you are . . . there."

"I will always be there," the Marquis answered, just as I know you need me, I need you, and, Heart of my Heart, that is a proper foundation on which to build a home."

"I . . . love you! I love . . . you . . ." Sabra breathed the words over and over again.

Then, as she drew his head down to hers, he was kissing her wildly and passionately.

She knew he was taking the stars from the sky to cover her so that their beauty and glory shone like a light.

Then the starlight became a fire.

As they burnt together with an ecstasy that was the glory of the Divine, Sabra knew it came from Eternity and would go on into Eternity.

For Real Love there is no End.

Barbara Cartland, the world's most famous romantic novelist, who is also an historian, playwright, lecturer, political speaker and television personality, has now written over 450 books and sold over 450 million books the world over.

She has also had many historical works published and has written four autobiographies as well as the biographies of her mother and that of her brother, Ronald Cartland, who was the first Member of Parliament to be killed in the last war. This book has a preface by Sir Winston Churchill and has just been republished with an introduction by Sir Arthur Bryant.

Love at the Helm, a novel written with the help and inspiration of the late Admiral of the Fleet, the Earl Mountbatten of Burma, is being sold for the Mountbatten Memorial Trust.

Miss Cartland in 1978 sang an Album of Love Songs with the Royal Philharmonic Orchestra.

In 1976 by writing twenty-one books, she broke the world record and has continued for the following ten years with twenty-four, twenty, twenty-three, twenty-four, twenty-four, twenty-five, twenty-three, twenty-six, and twenty-two. She is in the *Guinness Book of Records* as the best-selling author in the world.

She is unique in that she was one and two in

the Dalton List of Best Sellers, and one week had four books in the top twenty.

In private life Barbara Cartland, who is a Dame of the Order of St. John of Jerusalem, Chairman of the St. John Council in Hertfordshire and Deputy President of the St. John Ambulance Brigade, has also fought for better conditions and salaries for Midwives and Nurses.

Barbara Cartland is deeply interested in Vitamin Therapy and is President of the British National Association for Health. Her book *The Magic of Honey* has sold throughout the world and is translated into many languages. Her designs "Decorating with Love" are being sold all over the U.S.A., and the National Home Fashions League named her in 1981, "Woman of Achievement."

In 1984 she received at Kennedy Airport America's Bishop Wright Air Industry Award for her contribution to the development of aviation; in 1931 she and two R.A.F. Officers thought of, and carried, the first aeroplane-towed glider air-mail.

Barbara Cartland's Romances (a book of cartoons) has been published in Great Britain and the U.S.A., as well as a cookery book, *The Romance of Food*, and *Getting Older, Growing Younger*. She has recently written a children's pop-up picture book, entitled *Princess to the Rescue*.

BARBARA CARTLAND

Called after her own
beloved Camfield Place,
each Camfield Novel of Love
by Barbara Cartland
is a thrilling, never-before published
love story by the greatest romance
writer of all time.